Only in LA:
A Year in
the Life of a
Hollywood Trainer

Only in LA:
A Year in
the Life of a
Hollywood Trainer

A Short Novel Based on True Events

Eric Jorgensen

MOUNTAIN ARBOR
PRESS
Alpharetta, GA

This is a work of fiction based on actual events. In certain cases, incidents, characters, and timelines have been changed for dramatic purposes. Certain characters may be composites, or entirely fictious as product of the author's imagination. Some names, identifying details, and events have been changed to protect the privacy of individuals.

ISBN: 978-1-6653-0113-8 - Paperback
eISBN: 978-1-6653-0114-5 - ePub
eISBN: 978-1-6653-0115-2 - mobi

These ISBNs are the property of Mountain Arbor Press for the express purpose of sales and distribution of this title. The content of this book is the property of the copyright holder only. Mountain Arbor Press does not hold any ownership of the content of this book and is not liable in any way for the materials contained within. The views and opinions expressed in this book are the property of the Author/Copyright holder, and do not necessarily reflect those of Mountain Arbor Press.

Library of Congress Control Number: 2021916003

Printed in the United States of America   1 0 2 6 2 1

♾ This paper meets the requirements of ANSI/NISO Z39.48-1992 (Permanence of Paper)

Photo credit: Kris Jorgensen, Georgie Jorgensen, Sia Properso, Syd Wilder

June 4, 2021, Eric Jorgensen left our world to be with his father in heaven.

With what little time he had on this earth, he pursued a life with the purpose of spreading light, love, happiness, and a lot of laughter to the vast amount of people who crossed his path. Because of this, Eric changed more than health; he changed countless lives.

So in memory of the endless dedication he held for his family, friends, and clientele, we made it OUR purpose to continue his dream in getting this book published with hopes that Eric's legacy will live on forever.

Now, as his dream lays here in your hands, we ask you, the reader, to continue passing the torch that is Eric, and spread the same light that he once did in this world.

He will forever be in our hearts, until we meet again.

Eric's family,
The Jorgensens

Dedicated to my Blood Family and my Fitness Family who have kept me going all these years . . .

"There is nothing noble in being superior to your fellow man. True nobility is being superior to your former self."
—Hemingway

CHARACTERS/PLAYERS
(IN ORDER OF APPEARANCE)

Bro: Devon's brother, fire dept. chief, the kind of person who would give his Life for you

Calista/ Cali: A-list actor, her name means "Most Beautiful"

Jay: Devon's friend, and fitness colleague, "Man about town," Hustler/Promoter

Guru Chick: Amazingly compassionate acupuncturist and spiritual guide

Amanda: Bel Air actor, queen, diva

Wendy: Devon's ex-fiancée

Mr. Jones: Devon's client, notorious mgr. of Neiman Marcus

Devon: Professional fitness trainer

Linda: Devon's client, ball-busting, high-powered, studio executive

John: Devon's friend, A-list bodyguard, a "salt of the earth" kind of guy

Sammy: Devon's client, malibu mogul

Cindy/Cin: Devon's blonde, bombshell roommate

Vincent: Devon's client, Beverly Hills A-list hairdresser

Ryan: Devon's client, powerful, entertainment lawyer

Michelle and Bobby: Calista's daughter and son

Timothy: Lead actor in Calista's movie

Sheryl: Devon's client, Calista's friend, musician/rock star's wife

Brett: Devon's client, upcoming blockbuster actor

Tom: Calista's ex-husband, egomaniac, executive producer

PART I

LIFE

JAMAICAN VACATION FLASHBACK

The Caribbean breeze carries the mouth-watering aromas of jerk chicken and mango, which attack my senses like a rhinoscopy as our gorgeous, ebony waitress sets down freshly squeezed glasses of mango juice in front of us. The Rasta chef cooking on the open grille beside us keeps checking us out. I am compelled to choose to stare at the beige sand and the surreal, postcard-blue-green water as a tourist jet skier races by.

"What are you gonna do now?" my brother asks.

We have been evading reality by having a blast in Negril, Jamaica for a few days.

"I don't know, maybe give it one more shot!"

"Shot at what?"

The waitress brings our brunch of fruit and fish scramble, which is the national dish.

"I just want to help others still, maybe kids."

He looks at me and grins as if to say in a subtextual way, "Where did my real bro go?"

"No really, I am over it. Best year of my Life though. Made me see." I study his reaction as I bite into the Ackee and Salt cod. "Damn, this is good!"

"Ya Mon, great hangover food," he blurts out through a muddled mouthful.

He swallows his first, huge bite, pauses, and responds, "I believe you."

"Good, 'cause if you don't then who else will my brotha'?"

He smiles, and I glance again at the perfect beach. I take a deep, deep breath, and drift back to one more memory of the darkness that I came from as I see an all-too-familiar silhouette of a lovely goddess sauntering by the gazebo.

REALITY,
EXACTLY A YEAR AGO

FEBRUARY 22

The moment she walked into the place my head was spinning like a carousel out of control. I gasped, open-mouthed at the exquisiteness of her grace as she strolled, nonchalantly, through the room light as a feather but as present as a lioness. I secretly desired her from that very moment. I wondered if anyone could see my thoughts or were even able to fully see the beauty I felt in my soul before me then.

Her name is Calista. There she is again, right in front of me, checking in at the front counter of the gym, but I could not hear the words falling from her delicate lips. I was deaf to them, temporarily in an infatuated, fantasy coma, mesmerized. I forced myself to click back into existence and not stare impertinently wide-eyed as she glided by us for the second time.

The employee meeting in the foyer was over and the group started to disband. It had to be the first time that I wasn't one of the coworkers bolting away as if to escape some form of wrath prophetically destined to afflict us like a plague where we sat. I took a few long breaths to take it all in. Should I go and speak to her? Should I investigate this exalted Angel of intrigue or covet it from afar? My heart is still recovering from the last near-fatal blow.

The answer becomes clear as my patience and self-doubt begin to drown my inspiration. I exhale my desire as I let go of the moment, and start to walk away. Tomorrow will be a new day.

Just then, Jay walks over and slaps me on the back. I am wondering if he knows my intentions, or worse, thinking the same as me. I am instantly on my guard. My awareness is piqued for any stultifying sign of renewed betrayal. How pitiful my trust factor has become. I am a nursemaid to a smashed heart and a knife stabbing. The gash in my back is still gaping open from the last time.

I know, we all have those battle scars to deal with, right? I laugh now at my younger military days when I was unbreakable. You could hurl me against a wall and spit on me, and I would just bounce off and brush it off. What happened to me? I let a few people in, and now I am walking wounded! I wish I might have died a war hero instead. There is at least a modicum of honor in that depending on what your government's agenda is, and/or just simply fighting to keep the soldier next to you safe and alive. I am picking myself up by the bootstraps now and am such a baby with my sad stories of wronged woes.

I smile and patronize Jay in replying to his barrage of incessant questions of unimportance. I see his lips moving, but I hear not a word. Who is he to question me? Bastard. He is probably setting me up right now. I "shine him on" as my old college buddy used to say. Some people are so self-involved that they will actually fall for that ignorance-is-bliss routine. If they only knew the things that they don't know, it would probably give them a migraine just trying to keep up in a simple, intellectual conversation.

Calista leaves, and I feel her presence immediately gone, and as she drifts away, so does my energy. Fuck it.

"Jay, you want to go eat?"

We leave the parking garage on Sunset in his Range Rover, the LA status symbol of choice. Yeah, I Love it. Who knows when you might have to drive in light rain during a storm watch, do some curb-hopping, go through some treacherous muddy terrain or, heaven forbid, creep through a snow-packed street in the Hollywood Hills. Like that happens.

LA is the first time I ever had the cognition of "car personalities." It is too bad that people actually buy into the subconscious belief of "what kind of vehicle I drive defines me as a person." I wonder if Henry Ford ever imagined it would go this far. He was happy enough just to be able to transport his groceries from the market in an easier fashion, I'm sure.

I am not sure why, but for some reason we just don't seem to find this kind of cuisine in the Beverly Hills area. The mere thought of some vegetarian, Hollywood prima donna having to watch me eat oxtail, cabbage, rice, and beans on Beverly Drive makes me smile though.

Bittersweet reminiscence sets in as we blast old-school Rob Base & DJ EZ Rocks' "Joy & Pain" for fun. This is what Life is all about, living in the moment. I start to forget all about my pain, and for a second, I am once again totally free until Jay asks, "How is Wendy?"

My smile turns to stone. What the hell is he doin'?

"I think you should give her a present. It will free up that huge chip on your shoulder, yo."

What the hell does he know? If he had it his way, he would probably be f-ing her right now. Oh, did I say f-ing her? Yes I did. He doesn't Love her. Nobody could Love her like I do.

"What?" I yell back at him.

He turns down the music, "You will grow so much."

I'm thinking I could harness growing the world's biggest tumor over just approaching the bitch, let alone actually finding, purchasing, and giving her a present for her new baby.

This guy doesn't have a clue what he is asking me. I look at him like he just shot the president. I say nothing. My moment of joy obliterated by nostalgic demons. We get out and go in.

The other customers size me up. How often does an unfamiliar, white boy enter this establishment? LA is funny like that. In the space of about twenty minutes tops—depending on your mental map memory knowledge and traffic—you can go from Boys-town, homosexual Utopia, to pretentious Rodeo Drive, to Crenshaw and enjoy some absolutely beautiful Baptist Gospel, east to eat authentic, first-rate, Mexican cuisine, or to Chinatown for dim sum, and don't forget the cleanest beaches in the world—yeah right. Anyway, it is all here.

We order, and Jay pulls out his regular wad of bills, almost too big to fold over and fit back into his shorts pocket. I reach for my smaller stack of cash, but he stops me. He always has money because he is a promoter of all things that bring the green. He is a "man about town," a man who never has to wait in line at the club. The guy who knows everybody, and everybody Loves him, or so he thinks. Jay is a hustler, working certified as a fitness trainer, who wants to be a celebrity actor.

We are enjoying our eats, and I see Jay eyeballing a girl who just walked by, and he looks at me. I check out her big, round, firm, Jennifer Lopez-booty. We both smile and go back to gorging.

Jay gets plenty of chicas because "girls just wanna have fun" and party, and he is always at the center of things. Plus, he was the only boy in a large family of sisters, so he really, really knows women. Not to mention he has Idris Elba's good looks and speaks fluent French.

People in general just gravitate to him though. The first couple of times hangin' out with him, guys would always try to buddy up to him. I used to wonder why people did this and after about a week, discarded any preconceived perceptions with the quickness. Jay has enough charisma to fuel a whole platoon of jet fighter pilots.

I also found out from him that he went to an Ivy League school even though he never mentions it to anyone. He likes the element of surprise, I guess. He is usually one of the sharpest ones in the room, but most people would never know it, unless they crossed him . . .

* * *

I'm lying here. This Guru Chick is sticking needles in me, and I am actually paying her to do it. *Only in LA.* If you told me I would be doing half the stuff I have already done thus far after moving here four years ago, I would have laughed at you and labeled you with "crazy." This is what you do here. You find all these new things, and after a while you end up Buddhist or something. You go home for Christmas in "Realworld USA" and they look at you like you just got out of prison, or whatever.

While she puts her hands on me and assesses my level of sadness within, I think about today and why I have been dragging more than usual. How do you sleep when your heart is pounding, and your mind is circulating ruminations faster than the globe is spinning?

So, I listen to her, take some newfound herbs, and say, "What the hell." Hey, the Chinese have been kicking ass for years with this stuff. I *definitely* do not need prescription drugs or to be cut open traditional American style. Besides, it would take three weeks just to get an appointment for a referral, and at that point, that doctor would be dumbfounded as well.

I guess I could go to a headshrinker like all the rest of the neurotic, dysfunctional people I meet here with some form of "I made it" success. Personally, I prefer self-help. It is at your own pace, and you can diagnose your own progress without going bankrupt, or at least without establishing a new codependency.

It's over. She is pulling out the pins. I'm cured, at least until some dipshit cuts me off on the way home, and my potential road rage kicks in. Well, who am I trying to convince, you or myself?

* * *

I am driving in my Jeep to my sixth and last appointment of the day now. She is a typical Hollywood prototype. She takes drugs, drinks, smokes, doesn't eat, and wonders why all her plastic surgery is costing so much to cover up this really aggravating aging thing going on with her. "It is so weird how that happens," she keeps telling me.

I listen as if I empathize with her. She is having so many problems right now with her dog not being allowed to be in her next film and whatnot. Pooky, the mutt, eats and gets treated better than most US citizens.

Anyway, the aristocrat's name is Amanda. She is totally

harmless unless she doesn't get her way, of course. Will have more about her later.

Amanda kind of reminds me of what my ex would be like if she had survived here for another twenty years before she escaped back to the Midwest where she could reign supreme with her new LA savvy. Wendy is one of those untouchably hot models who think their shit doesn't stink during their 20s, but then age, gravity, and bad habits kick in, and they mysteriously become a bit more humble.

So, she only had a little more time to snag one of those multimillionaires that hit on her every day that she always says are her "friends," and "like her for who she really is." These guys can sell water to a well while they pull away in their Ferrari laughing, if you know what I mean. They feast like the Great Whites on the young, beautiful, naive, and lower-income babes, leaving only a shadow of a carcass behind.

The truth, well, I just got my heart shattered and pulverized. It's been a minute so, big deal, right? I thought so. As you all know and if you don't, God help you—broken-heart rehabilitation is a bitch. I can feel Zen one hour, and then the next, a dog could walk up to me and piss on my leg, and I would probably apologize for standing like a tree and thank him for the attention afterward. Unless it was a girl dog, and because of my crushed ego, I would then be afraid to talk to her for fear of getting bitten (i.e., hurt again). Her name, if you haven't guessed, is Wendy.

Wendy came from Ohio. Small-town girl enters illusion-filled Glitterville. I thought, *Hey, if we are engaged to be married and helplessly in Love, what could happen that we couldn't handle?* I looked up foolish in the dictionary, and there was my picture by it. She was the kind of girl that when she walked in a room, the whole place lit up, and that was when she wasn't smiling.

I had no idea what I really had. I just thought she had the whole package, and internally, she made me feel "complete." I didn't realize that every swingin' dick around that got to know her was jonesin' to ruin something so pure as a simple couple in Love. Jealousy and envy—Shakespeare was onto something huh? I should have taken that a little more seriously in school. Who knew?

* * *

I must be crazy. No, my client is crazy. Who else gets up at four a.m. to workout at five, every day of the week? Gotta Love him though. He is the nicest, most polite, and accommodating man I have ever met, even before his morning coffee. Me? I don't want to talk to anyone before my caffeinated cocktail of choice.

I kick his butt as usual. He is so resolute that he doesn't even grasp the concept of muscle fatigue. When he cannot do an exercise to a predetermined set of reps anymore, he thinks he is doing a bad job, or is weak. His parents must have been hard on him. Can you say "perfectionists," or "not ever good enough?" Poor guy.

I call him Mr. Jones. He is the person from Beverly Hills you are trying to "keep up with." This man will never quit. His mind just doesn't function that way. He is a bona fide driven individual who has worked for every penny. A winner in the game of Life. You either Love him or hate him depending on your own shortcomings and insecurities. He reeks of class, style, and earned respect.

The admirable thing is, he seems to treat all people equally. I am not sure if I would work for him under any other circumstances though.

Oh, I forgot to tell you; My name is Devon, and if you haven't figured it out by now, I am a professional fitness trainer. My day is a constant, nonstop, hourly jambalaya of gym to gym, house to house, beach to park, place to place, client to client, eccentric (rich) person to crazy (not so rich) person.

When I got out of college, I thought my education would propel me to new heights in this vocation. Little did I know that my most useful classes would be from the Psychology department, and if I had it my way, I would screen each new client with a signed stress and health questionnaire first before I even decided if it was worth it to put my integrity, or what is left of it, on the line.

Most of these people here have never done manual labor, much less the grunt work it requires to look like the cover of a fitness magazine. They think Manual is the guy who takes care of the roses and shrubbery in their unused yard. They have no clue what kind of commitment it really takes to have ripped abs at thirty or older, or to get that sexy, lower rectus abdominis muscle to be razor-edged and pop out like Brad Pitt's does in *Fight Club*. They just know that it is the one thing they don't have so they want it. Who am I to tell them they can't? Besides, they have money, so it entitles them to it, right?

I usually give them that, "If you are not successful then I'm not successful" line initially. I used to mean it. Everyone in LA becomes full of shit eventually. I swear it is an inevitable survival technique of imperative necessity around here. I didn't used to be this way though.

THE GENESIS,
THE EXODUS,
AND HOLLYWEIRD

I guess in the beginning, the appointments didn't seem to fade into all the others. When I started personal training in Portland, Oregon, it was because I truly cared so much. I just wanted to make a difference, somehow, in peoples' lives, but as time passes so does our altruism, I suppose. It seems to slowly blow away like dust layers being delicately brushed away on a new archeological find. I started at forty dollars an hour, which is a monumental income in some less lucrative countries, and an amount that left me ecstatic in 2002. That faded rather quickly, as it is human instinct to desire more, or at least believe you are entitled to it?

My phone rang one day out of the blue and it was my long-lost college roommate and buddy, Matt. I was elated and surprised; he invited me to a night on the town in LA on his dime for my birthday, on behalf of all the times I helped him out during our bread-sandwich and barely-able-to-pay-rent phases.

He said, "Hey I owe you. Come down to LA and we'll

hangout, on me, and by the way, I have somebody who wants to meet you!"

So, after asking Wendy for permission (we had just gotten engaged!), I drove down and found him training at his then-favorite dojo.

I walked in like a cripple from driving nonstop and proceeded to loosen up. The walls were lined with padding for my martial arts friend to crash or get crashed into. I watched intently as Nicholas Cage's kids were having a private lesson with him.

They bow and prepare to leave, and Matt comes over to me. "Hey thanks for waiting. How was your drive?"

"Not bad."

"Do you mind meeting someone who trains here? I told him about you, and he said he wants to meet you."

I nod in agreement as it seems like the polite thing to do.

"I told him to stop by about now after you called, so he should be here any minute."

As he turns to look out the back door, a shiny sports car rolls up. An average looking guy with shades on gets out. He walks up.

"You must be Devon."

"Yes, sir."

"Oh, wow dude, you can call me Frank."

"Nice to meet you, Frank."

He looks at me as if I am a new car he is about to purchase, and bluntly asks me if I would like a new job.

Another half-hour of interviewing and questioning passes, and he drives away after his proposition, and I am left with the "grass is greener/big fish in small pond" syndrome kicking me in the naïve ass.

He says he doesn't "trust" anyone there, and after talking to me, he wants me to move to LA and help him out training his base clientele of "celebs" while he ventures off and works with others on movie sets? I should be so lucky!

I go back to home base after a great couple days in La-La Land and commence to skillfully make my client's fitness dreams come true. I am full of wonderment and supposition as to whether I should make the Hollywood transition?

I feel so comfortable here. So far, my quest to implement health and fitness into working professionals' lives was going well, and I was feeling more bulletproof than when I was in the military. I trained with passion, like it was for the Olympics, and I was the embodiment of customer service. I did it all: nutritional programs, sports-training, pre- and post-natal, shoulder and cardiac rehab, osteoporosis/geriatric work, working with the marketing department at NIKE Corporate Campus, house-calls, etc., but I was also a reserved, introverted individual who was good one-on-one but terrible in crowds, and LA seemed daunting.

Wendy was the deciding factor. She didn't want to stay in the rainy Northwest. She said it made her "depressed." So, because I adored her and perceived it to be the ultimate blessing, we packed up our meager belongings and trekked out to the Promised Land.

But I felt insecure all of a sudden, maybe because I was scared? Scared of the unknown. That is what I feared. It is what we always fear. Whether it is under the blue, murky water, in the dark night, or in the future we cannot see.

After Operation Desert Storm in the Army, I vowed to conquer these and all fears, so I go to my church and pray. Upon leaving, I believed I must go. Take my humble self and break new ground. LA needs me. Yeah right, or so I thought. How genuinely green I was.

In Hollywood, on Beverly Street, I am excited to meet

and train my first celebrity client ever. I show up early and say a little prayer to the sky. I am nervous and could barely sleep the night before. He is late, and I am not used to this. My clients in Portland were very punctual.

He strolls in, and looks me up and down and says, "What, are you auditioning for a NIKE commercial or sumthin'?!"

"Hello, my name is Devon, nice to meet you." He doesn't even shake my hand. I look at the beautiful woman next to him to acknowledge her.

He sees this and as she walks away, he blasts me with, "That's my fuckin' wife!"

As if by looking at her I am completely disrespecting him, or her? I do my very best to make him happy, but it is painfully obvious that I am unfamiliar with the ease and disease of the "Hollywood Crowned Crowd."

He is suspicious of everything. I am uncomfortable the whole time. I cannot talk shop with him, as I know nothing of the business or anyone he brings up that's on the studio set he is shooting his television show or movie at. I don't even know what, or where, the studios are.

He is short with me and easily irritated by everything, as if he has been up for days and had ten pots of coffee, or whatever.

I feel like a failure as he says, "See ya whenever," and walks to his Porsche with his soap opera actress, trophy wife, peels out of the parking lot, and cuts someone off.

I go to the locker room to relieve myself and a guy introduces himself, and as I formally shake his hand, he steps in really close with his face and asks me if I "want to step into the sauna" with him.

He holds my hand a little too long, and I start to feel uncomfortable again, like a pet fish that just jumped out its bowl, floundering and struggling for air on a foreign plane. I just walk away. It's all I can muster. It isn't even lunchtime yet and this is getting weirder by the hour.

The next appointment is here. She is a psychiatrist who deals with some pretty big names around here, I have been told. She is very sweet, low key, and talks in a monotone voice.

Everything is going smoothly until right in the middle of an exercise, her eyes gloss over and she freezes up like a mannequin in the middle of the room.

She stays like that for at least two minutes, and it seems like eternity to me as I ask her over and over, "Are you alright? Is everything okay? Do you want me to do anything?!"

Finally, she comes to Life by shaking little vibrational shakes for about ten seconds, looks at me in complete embarrassment, and literally runs out the door with no explanation at all. I am nonplussed.

I follow her outside to make sure she is okay, and she screams at me to "leave her alone!"

So, I just keep on walking down the street as if I don't even know her. Was it an anxiety attack? Schizophrenia? *And she was supposed to be the normal one*, I thought, *counseling all the mentally and chemically challenged social misfits?*

* * *

I turn around and walk back to the gym after three city blocks of doing my utmost to let it all just roll off my shoulders when I spot what is probably the next appointment walking in.

He is a casting director, and I have to believe he is nice because he doesn't stop smiling at me, and frankly, he is the first one who has yet.

I start to train him when he asks to be stretched out by

me, and that that's all he really wanted today. At this point in my Life, I usually did not touch my clients. I am somewhat unsure and decide to show him a bunch of stretches upstairs in the empty aerobics room.

He asks, "Have you ever done any acting before?"

"No sir," I reply.

He retorts, "You can stop calling me 'Sir', Dave would be nice."

"Yes sir, I mean, Dave. No, I'm afraid I wouldn't be able to do that."

"Why not, I think I have something perfect for you. You could come by my office tonight. We will just have a few drinks and then you could try it!"

"I—I—I'm not sure, I have to pick up my fiancée from work. We only have one car—"

"That's okay maybe another time. You're the shy type, aren't you?"

"Umm, I—"

"I like it, it's cute."

"Umm, thanks?"

"Do you like to do Ecstasy?"

* * *

The first day was hell. It was also my first time being rejected at a house-call training session for a lesbian couple who, upon getting there on time in rush hour traffic, realized I wasn't gay. They decided I wasn't even close to being on their "team" as they reported to the owner of the fitness company who hired me for the day as a fill-in for them.

My only positive experience was training an investment banker when his trainer didn't show up. He was used to the old, traditional, weight-training workout, and I put him through a good one and was instantly hired. This guy wasn't even one of the clients I moved here to train. He ended up being my only normal experience that week as well.

Meanwhile, Frank was off on some exotic movie set in Europe, getting paid big bucks training only one actor, while I sat here fumbling my way through the day like an estranged idiot with his eccentric, neurotic, scheming, offensively impolite clientele.

I had never witnessed behavior like that before from any of my clients in Oregon. And this is how it was thus far on my first day in Hollyweird.

Frank came back from that on-set job, had a nervous breakdown when his live-in Mom passed away, and then mysteriously disappeared. Our incorporation was over as fast as it began.

They say we meet people for a reason, a season, or a lifetime. These people were for a reason, and as I made my way through the days in front of me like a blind person through an unfamiliar room, I found new clients and slowly became acclimated to my new environment.

I found the seasonal ones next and took a job at the newest, happening gym in town. After three years of initial LA hardship, I lost my old self and struggled to find the new one. Not the more reclusive, softer-spoken, hopeful one, but the now darker, cynical, embattled Devon. The Devon of today . . .

Back to Reality

I am waiting for my next victim as my Fitness Manager waves me over to his desk because he has decided that right now is the optimal moment to express his desire to hit goal this month, and give me the first degree about my sales, and how many hours I am currently training.

I give him the power speech of confidence to reinforce his lack of belief in us corporate worker bees. I tell him that I am "committed to roping in the big players for the cash."

Yeah right, the house takes sixty percent—and that is before taxes. What a joke! I would be broke while they keep ludicrously charging up to $150 a session. I wish he would have asked nicely and not pulled that used up power trip on me.

I give him a parting look of confidence as *she* walks by. I can feel her presence. It's Calista again, the screen goddess.

She doesn't even notice me. How bemusing. Usually, I at least get a glance from a woman. I am in my element, and want to go up and talk to her, but my anxiety is off the charts. I would probably end up eating my own tongue. This illusionary spell cast on me is a new nightmare of neuroses.

I leave the office as my manager is still mumbling

something about nothing and drift towards her. The nearer I get the more I start to choke on my overly analyzed, well-thought-out dialogue, so I lose my objective and abandon it like a battered puppy.

The past is still haunting my days even though I see all the possibilities but do not believe I deserve them. Who am I to fall in Love twice in one lifetime? Most people only find definitive, genuine, absolute Love once. Hence, "True Love," right?

Well, who the hell really knows? Someone who has, that's who, and at this point in time, it sure as hell is not me. In my elementary placement on this path of Life, I suppose this is another one of those lessons to learn. So be it!

While she sadly floats away from me, my next victim is waiting. He is in the best shape of all my clients. Why? Because he is gay, of course. His name is Kris. Sometimes I call him Krissy. He gets a little dramatic about that but under the surface actually Loves it.

Yes, it is true that the gay men in West Hollywood—or Weho—are probably the healthiest percentile group in America. What is funny is that aside from being queeny, or downright butch-scary looking, most of them will do anything to look good. I have straight clients who are tough as nails but when it comes to being completely consistent, following a menu for a nutritional program, taking proper supplements regularly, or using the needle (by their own choosing, of course), they drop the ball. I swear the gay demographic almost single-handedly keeps the health club industry booming around here.

I can tell what kind of workout we are going to have as soon as I see the level of effort and attitude I get in the first sixty seconds. Oh no, he is not going to be a COQ (Cranky old queen) and start that bullshit again about the fact that

we happen to end up using the bench press next to someone he loathes, though they slept with each other last
week. The shit I put up with. *Only in LA.*

* * *

I am driving in the Hollywood Hills off of Mulholland
Drive, trying to find a house in this maze of hairpin turns
and narrow side streets barely big enough for a go-cart.

The destination, if I can find it, is to meet a potential
new client. It is sort of like an interview. I have already
been referred to him, so I am in the loop.

In the movie industry—or at least dealing with, shall
we say, "privileged" people—if you are referred by someone of legitimate contact then you're in. It is like when
vouching for someone in the Mafia, and if you fuckup then
it's your ass. You won't be swimming with the fishes but
it's bye-bye reputation, and you will be even further down
on the food chain than the other wannabe "Star-makers,"
praying that someone will throw you a bone.

I find it and park. Now I have to go in, and if he likes
me, I'm the man. If not, then I am cast aside like a nerd-
clique reject in fifth grade.

You see, at this point, credentials do not matter. It is not
what you really know, or much what you look like either.
The very first week I moved here, I saw a guy training a
celebrity actor who looked like he just mowed the lawn
without a grass catcher and just strolled in to shoot the shit
for a while.

He wore beat-up, grass-stained, white leather shoes with
no socks, cut-off khaki shorts, and a plain white t-shirt. The
rumor was he had no technical training, education to speak
of, or prior experience to boast about either. In most cities,
this guy would not last a second as a professional.

In Hollywood, it is considered being down to earth and "real." I can see why though. Who are we to look better than an A-list movie star who just got out of rehab anyway?

Personally, I don't give a damn about that. I try to keep in as tip-top, kick-ass shape as possible because I want to be the example. I also make it a point to never ask anyone to do anything that I wouldn't do.

So, as I close my car door, I have my mini-Buddhist moment; take three inhales and exhales; try to embrace and appreciate the now; visualize success; find some Love of Oneness in my lost sense of self, and proceed. Who am I kidding? *Only in LA.*

I am greeted with apprehension at the door and a "who-the-fuck-are-you?" look from an overly protective assistant. I smile my biggest smile and try to think positive thoughts.

Everyone in this uber-modern, stilted house is probably riding this guy's coattails because they have no other meal ticket. The room looks like grade school with a few in a group whispering, and others scurrying around together as if they are too busy to say hello. I see them eyeball me though.

I hear him in the background. It is so sad to see everyone puckering up and being so dramatic as to do anything for him. If he asked one of them to bark like a dog or suck a fart out of his ass, they would do it.

By the way, how many assistants does it take to screw in a light bulb for a celebrity? One to hold it, five to help decide which light bulb is perfect, and ten more to collectively have enough will to overcome their fear of doing something wrong, much less, actually taking some f-ing initiative to screw it in!

So as soon as I get the opportunity, I am going to break

this guy down like the Army. No, wait. He is already a wad of chewing gum. I will do what no one else Loves him enough to do. I will help him empower himself. He will eventually be able to spit nails.

You see all these pitiful parasites around him want him, even if it is only on a subconscious level, to be dependent on them. They are the enablers, the cannibals, and the weak of Hollywood, feeding off the creative.

This guy wasn't this way five years ago when he moved to LA They say Hollywood breeds insecurity. It is so true. You have to have the back for it or you'll snap. Jason is a stud, a virtual Adonis. I, now, will have the job of helping him find himself for the first time again.

Of course, all the "yes" people will resent me because we will potentially become best buds as usual, but this is how it works. I will come in and do my best to help Jason free himself from his own mental demons, all the while getting him in the best shape of his Life, and unconditionally let him hopefully "be the change" for others to have the unconscious permission to do it as well. Addiction is a bitch!

Now if I could only follow through with my own words of wisdom for myself. Can you say "hypocrite?" How I long to be more integrally sound.

The elusive fact that he was in rehab was scrambled into oblivion by the best publicist in town, or so it seems. They even make me sign a confidentiality agreement (NDA) before I go into his room.

I walk in, and he is lying in bed. He says "dude" almost every other word. He is still stoned from something he is probably on in order to wean him off the other stuff, but we vibe, nonetheless.

He tells me he doesn't want to be too "big." I have to bite my tongue from saying anything such as, "Yeah, like that's going to happen" or "You've got to crawl before you can walk buddy."

People act, or think rather, that they are going to wake up tomorrow after one workout too many and be like, "Oh no, I got too big, it must have been that extra set that did it!"

The guy is as skinny as a pencil. I reassure him that I am aware that the camera adds fifteen pounds, that I have worked with film stars before, and that I know what he wants probably better than he does himself.

He concedes. I leave confident of future bonding with the real guy underneath the shell of his thin veneer he has been trying to use to protect himself. He will be fun to work with at least if he, hopefully, has an iota of discipline left. Better dayz, better dayz . . .

* * *

Next, I go to the movie studio. Which one, I cannot tell you. Let's just say a major one. I will attempt to ward off the advances of one of the most powerful executive producers in town while I train her in between phone calls and rude interruptions.

This is absurd and ridiculous. About every five minutes or less, her cell phone, which I am predestined to carry, goes off. She then proceeds to cuss like a truck driver and threaten whole families to make her point known at the volume of a loudspeaker.

All those not in favor, say "nay." People avoid Linda like I-405 during rush hour. Of course, if you are a subordinate and you call her Linda you might as well place your neck in a guillotine pronto because if you don't know her it is "Miss Chairman" to you.

I boss her around as much as possible. She Loves it. It is the only time a man, or anyone, tells her what to do. To actually have sex with this woman would be like testing a NASA space environment. Instructional overload. The room temperature would have to be perfect, and oh, "A little more to the left, okay? Now!"

She is a huge, chi-sucking vampire feeding on the martyrs. She will never find peace to fill that huge hole in her soul, much less reach a higher level of fitness with her ridiculously packed schedule.

In Portland, I used to train one of the best cardiovascular surgeons on the west coast, and he was on call twenty-four seven, but still not as busy as this maniacal woman.

Talk about multi-tasking. As one of my other client's mother says, "She might as well stick a broom up her ass and sweep the floor while she is at it."

Her father must have never shown her any attention, acceptance, or Love. I have to remind myself over and over to have compassion for her while she is viciously chapping her secretary's ass off between exercises. So here I am, holding her phone to her head while she spits on me barking commands like a general. *Only in LA*, see what I mean?

It is time for my workout now. Talk about a challenge. I ran earlier with a child prodigy from west Bel Air, at the UCLA track even though it was a nails-on-the-chalkboard, turtle-paced jog. You know the kind that is so slow it hurts your knees, and you are dying to just stretch out your legs a bit?

Anyway, after being in one three-quarters of the day, the last thing I feel like doing is going to the gym, but I have to do it. If you look or appear weak in LA, then you are perceived as just that. I am going to do my usual; a super-circuit routine to stay toned.

There is a word for you, "toned." It really means just lack of body fat. Such as there is no such thing as cold only loss of heat, nor darkness just lack of light, etc. "Toned" became the abused catchphrase for marketing agents to describe the next fitness gimmick to be shoved in your face.

In my book, that expression is not as bad as some of the others like "lengthening." They use that one to describe muscles for such things as Pilates. Now I must ask you, how can you actually elongate a muscle any more than it is when it is attached to a bone at both ends (origin and insertion point for those anatomically inclined)? Unless you are still going through puberty, the bone sure as hell isn't going to grow any longer and your genetics predetermine how your muscles will be shaped by the degree of fast-twitch, or slow-twitch muscle fiber you have. How else would an elite Ethiopian long-distance runner outperform a world-class Russian power-lifter at the Olympics and vice-versa? Think about it.

Wouldn't you know it? I work out at one of the most pretentious health clubs in town. Have to be seen. Legitimacy, you know. This place is a sociological subculture in itself.

The women here are practically untouchable unless the first digit in your bank account is followed by six or seven more. This is where all the models and aspiring actor/actresses go. They want to be seen but they also want to escape the potential onslaught of horny derelicts that try to pick them up in the straighter, and less exclusive clubs. They are the beautiful and they know it. All those who seek, crash and burn. They are the Angels of the earth blessed like the mighty Aphrodite for us to gaze upon.

Most of them are unhappy though. If you couldn't eat, had to sleep your way to the top, were always under physical scrutiny, and never looked at seriously as a person with more than skin-deep intelligence, then you would be unhappy too. Okay, a moment of silence for them. Boohoo, go on Dr. Phil and get over it.

Most of the young, magazine cover-looking boys are just posers. *Only in LA* would a guy wear sunglasses inside the gym while working out, and a freakin' beanie when it is eighty plus degrees outside.

The rest of the male models are practically escorts to the gay population, even when they don't put out, they get surrounded by the onslaught of hyper-sexual power mongers who want a new boy toy to complete their almost perfect lives. You develop a resistance to it after a while and start to even have a sense of humor about it.

Some trainers become defensive and are labeled homophobic which will get you nowhere in a business which boasts a commanding influence of so many gay men. You know what they say about that though? Let's just say that maybe their insecurity is hiding something. Not always, but can you say, "in the closet?"

I don't believe any rumors anymore though. For every straight stud is four gay men fantasizing that he is a metrosexual who is only three cosmopolitans away from being an uninhibited experimental deviant at happy hour. That is how those celebrity rumors start.

Nothing surprises me though because rumors sometimes start for a reason. In the closet, hell—with some they should say, "in the friggin' basement." "Keep it on the down low" has a new depth in Hollywood where they pay big bucks to have it all swept under the carpet.

As I walk to the treadmills there are friendly faces in the crowd who say hello or wave at me for PR (public relation) purposes. The players in the game here are all diplomats because who knows who will be "Somebody" tomorrow. If you haven't figured that out yet, then you are not really in the game. No one wants to be left behind or ignored. To be anonymous here in LA before fame sets in is like getting hit with a lightning bolt on a sunny summer day. Practically impossible.

My friend, the bodyguard, greets me with a caring smile. He reminds me of a pair of old jeans. No matter how long it has been since you wore them, they are always comfortable when you find them again.

John is a salt-of-the-earth kind of guy. He would give you the shirt off his back and not ask for, or expect, a thing in return, which is a rarity in LA. He still has ideals, values, and integrity after existing here for the better part of seven years.

He protects some of the biggest names in the movie, music, and believe it or not, law business. He got the job by disabling a would-be attacker with a gun at a cheesy La-La Land party with an A-list crowd. The word spread and now he is in demand.

He looks at me and grins as if to say, "What the fuck are we doing here?" I get on the bike next to him.

"How are you treating Life?" he asks.

"I am doing better," I say with a grin of subtext.

"Better? Okay, what's up? We should go get some sushi and talk shop. By the way, before I forget, I might have a new client for you."

"Don't talk about food right now, John."

"Anyway . . . I would say tonight but I have a gig."

"Can't anyway, have a date."

"Whoa, that's it! I knew sumthin' was up! Wow, this is a first. How long has it been?"

I blast him with, "Shut-up!" and then look around to see if anyone heard me.

"Who is she?!"

I grit my teeth and start to whisper, "Easy, we're in a cornfield, dog."

"So, who cares? Who is she?"

"She works here!"

"What? Oh, okay. Oh, I know!"

And we both say in unison, "The yoga instructor."

"Yeah, so keep it quiet, I am already pissin' off my own dock if you know what I mean."

"Cool."

We do are arbitrary sixty minutes of cardio and decide it is time to go. He has a commitment this evening, baby-sitting—I mean, watching over—a comedian who has death threats for infuriating one too many devout Holy Rollers with his abrasively blasphemous routine while on tour through the Bible belt. Whereas I am off to a rendez-vous with a long-time fantasy of mine: a booty call with a lovely, ethereal yoga instructor.

MORE PLAYERS

MARCH 15

It's early morning, and my client is huffing and puffing on the sandy beach of Malibu. I have to go a little farther west to get here, so I take my new, death-wish crotch-rocket. I can cut at least ten to fifteen minutes off my time weaving through stopped cars and passing everyone. I used to be a hater until it dawned on me that I was just envious of their freedom to go anywhere without stopping for traffic jams, and I jumped on the bandwagon, so to speak. One of my most self-indulgent joys is when I pull up to some guy who paid a quarter million or more for a car to feed his ego in, and I blow past him like he is standing still. I passed a girl in a brand-new Lamborghini the other day (or maybe that was David Spade in his yellow Ferrari?), but she was driving it like it was a ride for the old folks at Knott's Berry Farm. It is only the guys who drive cars like that in LA, unless it's someone like Rihanna, Missy Elliot, or Cardi B.

I am kindly pleading for my client to breathe deeply and, "C'mon, you can make it!" while my thoughts drift in and out to last night as we jog. I learned a new appreciation for flexibility from yoga, and I am not talking about in the mind either. I will be a newfound fan for Life. I secretly thank the Yogi gods.

My client begins to tell me about his troubles. I listen intently and concentrate on him because he sincerely is one of the most dynamically influential men I have ever known. If he wanted you gone, off the face of the planet, all you have to do is look at him wrong on the same day he eats some mediocre pasta. He picks up the phone and you're a goner. It is that simple.

When I come over to watch the NBA playoffs on his private big screen theater in his den, he kids around that if my team is losing and I have a big bet riding on the outcome that all he has to do is make a phone call. He does this with a thick Italian accent as he pantomimes picking up the phone and dialing the numbers.

The saying goes that there is a little truth in every joke, but bless his heart because believe it or not, he is one of the most endearing men you could ever meet. Everybody Loves this guy, or maybe it is just respect? Sometimes I cannot tell. All I know is if he likes you, you are treated like a king, and the funny thing is he somehow makes you feel very special. It is almost like being knighted or being accepted into a premiere as a celebrity when you are not. If anything happened to him, I swear I would go after them myself. I guess you start to feel like he is sort of a father figure.

We head back to his estate overlooking the dark-blue Pacific Ocean to share our blueberry-protein smoothies. Now is when we take an allotted breather between two men to philosophize about all the time we experience so quickly on this planet called Life.

I start with a quote from Aristotle about how "God moves the earth like the beloved object moves the lover." He finishes the whole ten-minute moment with, "Don't follow the herd or you'll end up stepping in shit." Then we schedule our next training session, and I ride off feeling as if I have truly made a difference in someone's Life today.

* * *

My roommate wants to meet for lunch at this exclusive, organic, vegan coffee shop on Melrose. The place is such a scene. The people sit around, and every time someone walks up to the place it is like "up periscope," and they all stop to glance at the new body taking up space. It is worse than driving by an accident on the highway where everyone slows down to see the destruction and carnage.

Yes, celebs do frequent the place, so I guess it is a tourist/wannabe/curiosity overload kind of thing. A direct reflection of the thrust of celebrity sensationalism into our lives by the social media whores.

She walks up, all dolled up. Her name is Cindy, or "Sindy," so we just call her Cin for short. She is a super sweet, blonde bombshell, "tig ole bitty," Christian bible-thumping, stripper chick. How's that for a seemingly walking contradiction? *Only in LA*. She is fun to know but hard to talk to sometimes.

"What would you like to order?" the waiter asks.

"I just want a mocha, and whatever she wants."

After what seems like an hour of decision and questions like, "Do you have dairy free milk?" or "Oh is the soy certified organic?" or "And is your soy non-GMO (non-genetically modified)?" and "is the cheese rBST and rBGH free??" She knows this stuff is bad because the Whole Foods people told her, so it must be true. WTF? The air we breathe in LA has more contaminants in it!

To top it off, after asking for specific sweeteners like Stevia or Xylitol for her coffee, she begs me to share a normal, sugary dessert item with her! I assume it is so she doesn't eat the whole thing and feel guilty for breaking her nonstop, Life-long, everyday diet, but it is that time of the month and she has to have chocolate, or she will die.

"No!" I tell her.

She gives me that pouty look of pain.

"Okay then," as I look away, and my impatience forcibly dissipates.

I am such a sucker. No, all men are such suckers. Every guy on the patio is checking her out because they can't help it. It is just human nature, but they just don't realize what I have to put up with to get along with her. Talk about estrogen and mental overload. Sometimes I think she has only ten brain cells and they are all fighting. If it were only that, I would definitely consider her as a potential girlfriend. As it is, I could possibly go insane. Her caller ID name on my phone comes up as HM (high maintenance).

Cin at least listens to me when she asks for advice, is as cute as a button, and would do just about anything for me—even though her idol is Paris Hilton, and her miniature dog is always dressed in pink.

She is the kind of girl who cries if she sees a stray animal but would not go out with a guy if he didn't know what a Louis Vuitton bag was. People in parts of the world are starving, but she would never eat leftovers. She knows all the Mercedes Benz models and how much they cost but can barely balance her checkbook. Has a showroom model Mercedes CLK but doesn't know how to pop the hood to check the oil in it if the light, heaven forbid, actually came on. You get the idea.

I finish my quality time with Cin that she so desperately wanted to share with me because she needed help deciding whether or not to get liposuction on her perfectly curved hips by her father's plastic surgeon practice, and if I will give her a ride to the airport tomorrow when she leaves for her vacation to Greece for a week. I gladly say yes, thinking of the fact that I will be free of her for a week of sheer quietude, and promptly depart as she has no sense of time.

* * *

It is time to get my mop-top chopped again, so I stop by to see one of my clients for the task. This guy serves the crème de la crème of Beverly Hills. He is like an artist who goes to town like Edward Scissorhands and creates with raw instinct.

If in need of a new look, or you are having a bad hair hour and it is causing you major anxiety, then he is the man. Of course, depending on your personal status, you may have to control those insecurities for a day or three because he is most assuredly booked up for the week.

I, feeling like royalty, casually slide in there between those waiting because I am concerned about this guy's health and make him look "fabulous" when nobody else really gives a damn.

What is amazing is how much these top stylists are disclosed and the people they become connected with. Let me tell you, every personal trainer should train a stylist or two. It is good for business. Can you say "mega-networking?"

I walk in and see the frenzy before me. If I watch long enough, I will get to see someone have a drama-panic-diva attack over a new cut. It will pass, but they act like someone just died right in front of them.

I sit and watch the unconfirmed pieces of information fly at each conversational station. You can almost see the gossip floating from one mouth to another as if the words were literal darts of derogatory thought piercing the air.

It's my turn to be sheared. I, pleasantly, sit down in the chair which has been, nicely, warmed-up by some hot prima donna's ass from the Palisades. Looks like an actress or wannabe model. Hell, she could be a TV anchorwoman for all I know. They all look the same these days.

This is the place where the sexy, disheveled look was patented that everyone was trying to master. It is so ironic to see that look at locations like a well-known hotel pool on Sunset. The posers show up looking so perfect with this fake, slept-in look and/or perfect makeup, only to order a diet coke and salad and be seen, when you know it took them an hour or so to look that way, only to become the item of pretension itself.

Vincent is exhausted. His eyes look sunken and dark with circles. It is probably from listening to all those self-centered, energy vacuums today. I empathize for a moment because of the parallel with my occupation.

Even great trainers come in second to a hair appointment, sometimes to a mani/pedi, but usually first to a massage therapist or chiropractor.

He finally confesses that he was up partying for the birthday of the wife of a main studio executive last night, and that they are both his clients. Now I don't feel so sorry for him. Nonetheless, he rocks, regardless of his sullen state.

I tell him, without lacking any authority whatsoever, to go directly home, take some 5-htp (hydroxytryptophan), slam a glass of water with an Emergen-C in it, and crash for the night. He agrees with me in his almost-slurring French accent.

I am done and feeling fresh and new. Whatever, at least I am trying to keep up my image in this vicissitudinous city of some of the vainest vain.

Clubbin' with Jay, and the Calista Intro

May 2

Jay rolls up in the Rover and scoops me up. Tonight, we are going to a new, hot, hip, happenin' restaurant that he has a piece of. He tells the girls that he meets that he is the owner, and they fall for it. The truth is that he has about 2 or 3 percent ownership, give or take a few points. Hey when in Rome, or whatever works right?

It opened only a month ago, so it is still freshly coasting on novelty but after that, it could go tits up in the blink of an eye. I guess a lot of really big celebs have been frequenting the place. P'Diddy even showed up with his entourage for some Italian in the back corner VIP table last weekend. Rihanna, Ansel Elgort, some Kardashians (or Jenners?), and Jennifer Lopez were in this week as well.

It is on like Donkey Kong, and we are dressed to impress, bling-bling and all! Jay will be everyone's friend tonight, and I will be his sidekick.

I'm not sure why he even brings me along all the time. It has to be that I tend to do well in social situations and conversational settings. I dress and carry myself well. I was raised to be respectful and cordial to others and have good manners. No matter how wealthy someone is, if they are new money they can lack tact. I obviously don't come from either, but I was raised to have good etiquette, and the rest I picked up along the way through all those stuffy dinners I have been invited to over the years.

Don't get me wrong, no one out on the town in LA gives a shit. Who you are, what you are driving and flossing, and who you know always takes precedent. Personality always wins and confidence rules, but it is good to have some class or you will look like you are frontin' all the time. Intelligent people see through that and think that is weak or simply being a douchebag.

Maybe Jay keeps me close because I am the only one he actually trusts? It seems people tend to trust me right away. My dad abhorred dishonesty more than anything else in the world. If you lied to him, he could become a monster. When I was young, if I told a lie and he found out, he would tan my hide but good. I learned quickly not to even try him. Eventually, I was so scared to lie about anything to anyone that even if an accusation was based on circumstantial evidence, I couldn't do it. "Yep, I did it!" that was my motto as a boy if I messed up.

If you combine that with the fact that I was baptized, forced to be Roman Catholic, made holy communion, became confirmed, and was an altar boy (unmolested, thank God!), then you can imagine the guilt factor I would have to carry growing up if I did lie. It was conscientiously less grueling to just take my punishment and get it over with.

I guess I naturally tend to put out a slightly naive, sincere quality with people right away. Why else would clients ask me to house sit their multi-million-dollar homes;

drive their unused leased cars after they buy a new one; train their trophy wives and partners; hang out with and watch their kids; dog or cat sit; have gate codes, keep keys, and garage door openers to their residences to get on their property?

"What's up kid. What's crackin'?" Jay says as I jump in his Rover.

I can't even get out a word before his phone starts to blow up. When we hang, he is on the thing nonstop. I just kick back and enjoy the ride, the ride to the place and the ride we are going to go on that night because when you hang out with Jay you never know whom you'll meet, where you'll end up, and when the party will end.

I have spent many a morning doing the walk of shame to my car in the same threads that I left with the night before. Once I woke up in a limo, one time in Vegas, and one morning in San Francisco. Hell, one afternoon I woke up in a huge condo off of Wilshire with two of the hottest Brazilian women I have ever seen, in the same bed on each side of me, and I couldn't really remember what exactly went down. All I know is I had a smile on my face for a week after I recollected the happenings. I owed Jay one for that night.

The only thing said to me on the short ride to the valet out front is, "Yo, check out this new jam I picked up while I was in NYC, dog."

Valet is a joke. After we got out, they just drove it to the other side of the Melrose and parked. "That'll be twenty because we kept it close."

"Whatever," I pay him, and we go to the front door.

We completely bypass each line that makes you have to universally "wait." First you have the wait for the line to get in. Then the line you have to wait to get into a table, which transfers into the wait at the bar. For that wait, there is the line to get up to the front only to have to wait on a bartender to hook you up.

The only time I get peeved from this preposterous process is when the "door-whore" at a place acts like he can't let you in. Then randomly, I always see someone I know, and they say "hello" (like an owner or a client or whoever), and the guy acts like we share the same mother and calls you "homie," or "bro" when you leave. It makes you want to drop kick the beady-eyed bastard. It is his only hour of power, so he abuses it. He is also the one who makes you wait when the place first opens so they can create a line for the rest of the passing world to see to present perceived interest.

I have learned that you are asking for this treatment if you don't bring hot girls (more than two), know the right hookups (for the list), are with recognizable names and faces (famous people), and/or aren't rolling up in a Bentley and slingin' major cheddar (cash) around. Even then there is no guarantee.

This place we are hitting tonight is an eatery, and a much finer establishment than that, but that is usually how the restaurant/bar/club scene works. And believe me when I say everyone on a guest list thinks they are the most important person in the world, and that is before they start soaking up that alcohol. Too many of those in a room, and fools become exalted to demigods in less than an hour. That's how gunshots in parking lots can happen.

Jay walks in, and he gets Love from the hostess (a hug and kiss), Love from the manager on duty (handshake), and Love from the bartenders (a high five from the bar and two drinks served within three minutes tops, no charge).

"That's how we do," Jay toasts me.

I simply reply, "We are not here for a long time, but a good time."

We drink, and I give the room the casual once over, and I see her.

I turn to Jay and at the same time he says, "There's your girl."

I am speechless with a smile as big as Alaska. Calista is sitting in a corner power booth next to the front window with some girlfriends. They all are fine, but I lock onto her with my eyes like an f-14 fighter pilot and have to force myself not to stare.

"Calm down, Tiger," Jay says as he elbows me. "I'll be right back. Flirt with the nonnatives over there and don't even glimpse at her."

Then he almost palms my face and looks me right in the eye as he says really slow, like he's talking to a fourth grader, "I'm gonna hook you up," and he disappears into the sea of people.

I look over my shoulder to where he pointed, and there are two, really pretty, young girls glancing my way. They look like newly imported dilettantes. I almost blush. Any skills I may have are in severe, pathetic, atrophy. I lack the ability to make small talk. My passion is usually a slow, controlled IV drip, but lately it is so intense, it just gushes. All I can do is give them a big smile. It works though as they wave and start to inch closer. I know I will not actually panic, but I can't believe how despicably nervous I am.

Right as they get to me, I feel Jay's hand on my shoulder, and he blurts out, "How are you doing this evening ladies, can we get you another Grey Goose and cranberry?"

They look at each other, smile, and nod yes, in unison. Jay puts two fingers up and points overhead at the girls' drinks with the other hand and the bartender, Tim, comes over to serve us. We introduce ourselves and then Jay tells them that we will be at a table in the front for a while, so if they get bored why don't they come over and have a bite with us. They give us each a girl handshake, and we are escorted to our table immediately by the exquisite hostess standing by.

I almost forgot about Calista, because those girls at the bar are cute as hell, until we start to pass by their table.

Jay places his hand on my chest and whispers, "Slow down, I want to introduce you to someone."

I'm thinking that he is altruistically looking out for me, forgetting that Jay has an ulterior motive for just about everything he does. He casually stops and turns towards their table with his six foot three, linebacker-size bravado.

"Hello ladies, are you having a good time tonight. I am one of the owners, and I just wanted to make sure that you get . . . whatever you need."

Now, if the wrong guy says that with the wrong tone to the wrong woman anywhere, let alone LA, he will get shut down so fast that his closest kin would feel it. I, at this moment like so many before, am starting to get especially weak in the knees because I know I am going to have to talk to her now.

Calista retorts with poise, "Whatever we need? I might have a request for an after-dinner dessert. Who is your friend hiding over there?"

I am in complete awe. I have to check to make sure my jaw is not on the floor. She has obviously been putting down a few with her friends because they giggle like little schoolgirls when she stops. Calista has not missed a beat though.

"We are celebrating my birthday!" she says it as if the whole world should stand up and cheer and do a stadium wave.

Jay almost cuts her off, "Oh, so you're a Taurus. Well then this is someone you need to know. Maybe he can read your palm as a little sumthin'-sumthin' present, and later we can all go dancing."

I am still in shock! I don't know how to read palms, what is he doin'? Later, when I wake up from this dream, I realize he was just trying to create a smooth opening to flirt with her. Make contact.

"That would be nice, maybe we will have to take you up on that offer, but it looks like you already have company," as she points to the two girls from the bar walking up to us. "But it was nice to meet you."

Jay turns to me and gives me that look. The look that if I don't take advantage of the moment, he is going to disown me like a father to an abused stepchild.

"Nice to meet you," I say as smoothly as possible as I inch closer and reach out to shake her hand. I keep deep eye contact, and try to look at her like she is a giant peach I am about to devour, but inside I am trembling at her prowess and beauty.

She holds out her hand. I lean forward, and firmly pull it towards me with both hands, and gently kiss it as sensually as possible on the knuckles and then slowly start to leave. Hey, just because my crushed ego and nerves stop me from speaking smoothly doesn't mean I have no moves physically. I seem to run like a finely tuned formula-one racecar in that department.

"Hey, Mr. Man, what's your name?"

Wow, she actually is interested enough to ask. I turn back and look at her with as much cockiness as I can momentarily muster.

"Hi, I'm Devon but you can call me . . . anytime."

What a blundering mouthful of garbage, all you had to do was say your damn name!

"Okay, Mr. Anytime, I might . . . I just might."

They all laugh. I can't take her seriously anyway because I am practically shot in the ass by Cupid already. It is so surreal that as I walk ten feet to our table, where Jay is already making the girls crack up, I have to pinch myself to see if I am awake.

Calista is a major movie star. She is in all the tabloids, and guys are willing to throw themselves in front of a bus for her, and after seeing her up close I can see why. She beats the crap out of that "good from far but far from good" line. She has some serious Hollywood clout and status. I don't really care, or at least I don't think I do. There could be some placebo effect going on. I am prone to it just like everyone else, but I see so many celebs that I would like to believe I would not fall for the illusion of fame.

Nevertheless, I have never been so irrepressibly smitten by any woman or met one so impressive. In my universe, she just eclipses all others but to my heart, she seems just as dangerous as she is irresistibly sexy.

I sit down at the table, and Jay gives me that look. The look I was trying to avoid. Hey, I believe I should get a merit badge for my performance. It took all my courage to do that.

He leans over and whispers, "She is watching you right now so do not look. Flirt with these girls, you can close the deal when she goes to the loo. I'll let you know, dog." I start to shake my head, no. He kicks me under the table and says, "Strike while the iron is hot, my brotha'."

Well, that never happens, and I end up kicking myself thinking I will never get another chance like that one again, and of course Jay rubs salt in the wound daily for at least a week.

Truthfully, I don't know what I would do with her anyway. Why would she hang with me? I don't have much to impress her with, and I am too weak to just hit it and move on if indeed she was even the type, which I seriously doubt she is. She probably gets wined, dined, and porcupined by the biggest names and richest guys in the world. Oh well, I will always have my crush. Most guys would jump at the chance just to meet her, let alone kiss any part of her anatomy like I did. Can't really brag about this one though. No one would ever believe me.

* * *

We get our eat on and bounce to one of the hottest night spots in town. We valet in front, and the promoter, James, greets Jay, who inconspicuously slides him a quick, slide-of-hand transaction of whatever, and escorts us in, high-roller style.

It is a familiar scene, a zoo of nocturnal animals. It is where the hustler hip-hop crowd meets young rich Hollywood, and they all front, or think, they are ballers.

The rich kids think they are tough and invincible because they have fly cars and listen to rap, but they haven't experienced any real hardships to speak of. They are just a bunch of sheltered wannabes.

The A-list, and up-and-coming B- or C-list, celebs come in to feel special among everyone else and get some fake street cred by rubbing elbows with the thugs, and in return they get to try out their game on the celebs. Those in the middle beware. They are the prey for the evening.

I was somewhat used to this scene before I moved here because I used to be a bouncer at a high-end bar while I was in college that a lot of the high rollers would frequent. It was mindless work, but it helped pay for the room and board for a while.

I thought I had seen it all, but this place takes the cake, no pun intended. Girls here will do almost anything once they get some blow or E. The eighties were the coke era supposedly, but it is still the drug of choice for most. Even if they start on ecstasy, they will ask for the powder later on in the night. If it is their first time, forget it. It's all over. They will be doin' some crazy shit before morning. It will be like Vegas up in here, where it is just an excused write-off for their first offense, and a memory from the "things everyone has done and I haven't done yet but will try at least once" list.

James takes us into the back VIP room where there is an up-and-coming rapper, the owner, and about six scantily dressed girls sitting around in a plush room contoured like someone's backyard, peanut-shaped swimming pool.

The walls are all curved, have crushed maroon velvet, and built-in TVs. I notice the white, shag-like, fake fur on the ceiling when a girl who is obviously on E can't stop petting it overhead and moaning about how soft it is while her twin friend keeps writing her name on it with her finger. They wouldn't be able to even reach it if it weren't for the four-inch stilettos they are strutting around in. Nice calves though.

We meet and greet as usual, where each one of them has their own special vibe and handshake to go with it. The room looks somewhat like an MTV video: The rapper in matching team-sports gear and sideways hat but no entourage; the owner in Euro-jeans, cowboy boots, a designer T-shirt, and a flashy leather jacket; and us in suits.

The owner orders us a round of drinks from the waitress, and before you know it "the stuff" comes out. I have been there. I have gone to the dark side once out of peer pressure back in the day and endured a sleepless night where all I wanted was for my heart to stop beating like a kick drum and my restless brain to shut down like the sleep mode on my computer. Those few experimental days have long passed. I don't like that empty feeling the next day that you get. I have more than enough other mental and spiritual weaknesses to conquer and improve upon.

I purposely let it pass, and everyone looks at me like I am Five-O, or Po-Po, or vice, or whatever else you want to call the cops who try to infiltrate and bust these vampires every once in a while.

Before I moved here, I would crumble under such adult peer pressure, but now I just look them straight in the eye and tell them that the stuff fucks me up and I would rather roll a blunt, and then they drop it because in the hip-hop world, the green is king and all the other designer drugs are mainly for the chicks.

Although, if you drop a line like that, you better be holding (even though I am not because I don't smoke) or your perpetrating might get you stomped. People get paranoid and stupid once they start stimulating their cortex with mind-altering substances while swimming around in this underground vortex.

I break the tension by telling a joke. Everyone laughs and then I just order another drink. We stay and get buzzed while the girls start dancin' to the beats. It becomes a mini strip joint as more clothes start to come off, and progresses into a thong-along, "shake that back," twerk contest for us to watch.

No one touches the others' girls though. Good way to get beat down. At the end of the night, we are all going our separate ways with a smile on our face. That is the only way it should be. The haters and stupid, drunk, angry people are the ones who can ruin it for everybody. They are the debilitating amateurs. True pros of partyin' keep it real because they know it is just for good times, letting loose, and trying to find a honey for some potential belly-rubbin' lovin'.

A FULL
TRAINING DAY IN LA

MAY 12

Today is one of those mornings when you wake up and dread the overwhelming day's events because you know there will not be a second to rest. So, you fall back to sleep, only to wake up again and be forced to get up because there is no more time to procrastinate.

A week like this is when every day seems to run together in a blur. Kind of like those messy watercolor paintings you did in grade school where everything on the paper turns to the shade of a nice, brown hue of shit. Okay, maybe it is not as bad as that. I have my health, and I am helping people change their lives, and I'm busy right? Yeah, tell that to a corporate CEO or a studio head in this town and see how far your altruism gets you up the ladder.

The problem—I mean, challenge—is I don't live for power, or making the almighty greenback like someone with a greed obsession. Maybe I should be? I mean, on eBay today, a person in this privileged part of the world was willing to pay up to five thousand dollars for a piece of spat out chewing gum from a famous, teenage, Disney celebrity when there are a few decent charities or impoverished places that could use some help in the world.

Enough already, I am once again lost, desperately seeking to find humanism and the day hasn't even started yet.

I stop for my morning jolt. America's new cigarette: the morning, noon, and night espresso. I'm wondering if years from now, we'll see newly discovered evidence that caffeine causes premature, nervous system impairment. And when we do, this data, of course, will be covered up by all the food conglomerates and the coffee chains that even teenagers hang out at now for their fix. Laugh now, but caffeine is in everything these days. They even have caffeinated water on the market. No real flavor, just the alkaloid stimulant. Might as well just snort some methamphetamine too. Just joking, but it's pretty desperate when you think about it.

I often run into one of my clients inside the Starbucks I frequent. They all need their pick-me-up like me. I twist their arms off to get them to quit all the normal vices (i.e., overeating, undereating, drinking, smoking, drugs, etc.).

I even tried to quit coffee, but waking up at three, four, five, (and if blessed on a few days out of the year) or six o'clock in the morning and being the Mr. Happy Motivator for everyone you come in contact with year after year, it becomes somewhat difficult. They depend on you to boost them up, be high energy, and have a PMA (positive mental attitude) all the time.

I am still in a fog as I space out while in line. I am practically yelled at because I have not told the latte-god — who is really just pissed off because he hasn't sold any of his shitty scripts yet — my caffeine concoction of choice.

I give him the prompt, frank reply of my usual, everyday pick to let him know that it hasn't changed for years now,

"Grande drip in a venti cup please." This is why I might have to start Tai Chi again.

* * *

The gym is humming today. The LA crowd doesn't get serious about looking good for the summer until it is mid-April because: 1) They are probably in tip-top shape, or already striving to get there, and are as close as they are going to get in this lifetime; 2) They forgot summer was coming to this seasonless land because it is practically sunny every day; 3) Most of the poser models have stopped wearing their stocking cap/beanies during their workouts; 4) They wake up and realize as if it's an epiphany that, "Oh my God," or "Dude—like, pilot season is coming!" or; 5) They just recovered from their annual winter plastic surgery and/or liposuction travails.

Don't be so hard on them. Liposuction takes a lot of energy to recover from you know, but the hard part for me is if I cannot get them to change their root challenges (i.e., cardio, diet, etc.) then the surface problem arises again. Do you know what a fifty-year-old woman's arms look like if most of the fat cells have been removed from her hips and thighs at age thirty-five or so, and she gains an average of two pounds a year? When she waves hello or goodbye to you, she will most likely knock someone out with the arm flab if they are standing too close behind her. Everyone these days seems to have a Peter Pan complex and wants a shortcut to enhance their narcissistic needs.

I Love the positive vibe of the gym, but I look around and all I see are stereotypes: there is the exerexia chick on the Stairmaster, who looks like you should toss her a candy bar because she is way too thin. If she turns sideways, you can barely find her, and she looks sickly; crowding up the area is the spinning clique. They are like groupies to the spinning instructor. It is so "cute" how they ritually gather together for their shoe changing ceremony, coffees in hand, talking endlessly about God knows what; there are the mid-morning model/soap-opera actresses who can't quit staring at themselves in the mirror, or to see who is paying attention to them. This disables them from doing no more than a single set every five minutes. They always have to have a trainer when they work out because they require that much attention in order to, even motivationally, get to the gym. They are fifteen minutes late every time and can't resist babbling about their new starvation diet and skin revitalization products they got at Bloomingdale's yesterday; the Weho muscle boys who gather like high school cheerleaders, hug and kiss each other, and hardly even break a sweat in their skin tight workout wear from LA Sporting Club or the Lululemon store; can't forget the yoga crowd who sit serenely before class in their flip-flop sandals and discuss the removal of the blocking of their third chakra, certified organic foods, and how parasites in your sushi can be eliminated with a colon cleansing; the Napoleon-complex guys who either ridiculously shows off by attempting to lift way too much weight, or absurdly try to train their girlfriends and get into fights with them because they ignorantly stack on the excessive weight for them as well; and lastly, I see my own kind—the trainers.

You see LA is super saturated with trainers of all shapes, sizes, knowledge (or lack thereof), and experience (underrated). Most of them (myself included), have a shelf Life of limited years for many reasons. The burnout rate is high because of the aforementioned energy output, and the fact that you only make money per hour, so it is structured to have a ceiling of income. In other words, you can conventionally only make so much money per year, and then there is no room for upward mobility as a single proprietor.

Secondly, in LA (such as Miami and parts of NYC), youth is king. Health is attributed to the aesthetically good-looking or why else would we have those chiseled models on all the covers of our fitness magazines? And as you are more than aware, I'm sure that tends to fade as we age, therefore, depreciating the trainers' value, especially in Hollywood.

No one around here wants to pay an unattractive, out-dated trainer for his/her services. They want the best, hottest, coolest, newest trainer to shake up the scene.

Most trainers worth their salt are not entirely stupid, and they finally realize this somewhere along the way and look for an out, or they already have a plan. The plan may be solid, or the plan may be a fantasy. Winning the lottery is one. Inheritance is another. Maybe going back to college for a new career, or that late night real estate get-rich plan.

These are the glory days of training though. Sooner or later, it will be legislated just like all other professions that require technical schooling and licenses, other than just certifications.

Personal training was a respectable occupation, in my book, until it started getting whored out by the gym franchises and watered down by corporate greed. It used to be exclusive and now every Tom, Dick, and Harry thinks they know everything about working out, health, and nutrition so it entitles them to get a quick certification and go to work. Now it is like working at a fast-food chain and planning your next move to really make it big. Hence my next, final point.

In Hollywood, everyone is an actor or actress. I look around the gym this morning and see the quirky groups that come here, but the trainers themselves (at least most of them that are good-looking) think they deserve a license to be artistically inclined to act for the big bucks, or worse, fame. It is expected to go to a restaurant in this town and run into a cliché, but most of my clients would throw up on the spot if I announced one day that I am now a thespian, or artiste, with creative endeavors. Nonetheless, it is true that almost all the trainers I see before me this morning are actors in the making or breaking, with visions of grandeur. Hey, I have been on a few TV shows, movies, and a reality game show myself since I've lived here, but the truth is it doesn't pay my bills. I mean, I fixed my sink, but it doesn't make me a plumber. *Only in LA.*

* * *

Mr. Jones is right on time for his torturous treatment. I am in a hard-charging mood today and dialed, so this is going to be a no nonsense, no bullshit, no attitude workout. Not that Mr. Jones's temperament would ever allow himself improper things of this nature in the first place. We start with pushups. Most people I start training don't even know how to do a push-up correctly. They use their shoulders, round their back, and go too fast to properly flex their subscapular and pectoral muscles.

So, you can imagine how bad most peoples' form is in the gym. Sometimes a member's form is so bad, us trainers have to laugh and wonder, "are they making up a new exercise?" I can stroll through the place and walk up to just about every single person working out and give them tips on movement tempo and proper biomechanics. I can even do it for a person who has bad running form on a treadmill. I can't save the world one person at a time at the gym, but I can prevent these people from injuring themselves because it happens eventually if not corrected.

Mr. Jones finishes his warm-up, push-ups, and stretches, and we are off. Forty-five minutes of nonstop action. My clients don't waste a minute. They will never say they wasted their time with me. I am not the one. You will not be on cruise control on my shift and sweating is not an option. You will sweat!

* * *

He is here a few minutes late, which is very, very rare.

"Good morning, Kris, how are you, did you have a good weekend, do anything fun?"

"I was in Palm Springs. Remember? I went to that birthday party. Oh my God, I had the best massage from the cutest guy. I think I'm in Love!"

"Really, well that's great, thanks for sharing. So did you do your cardio, and not drink?" Silence follows with a look of distaste. "I'll take that as a no. That's fucked up. You promised."

"Oh, get off my back. I was having fun."

"It sounds like you were already on your back, so I don't know why you wasted your breath with that one."

"Fuck you . . ."

"Okay, then . . . Well let's get started, shall we?"

"Yes, let's bitch."

"Thanks. I learned from the best."

I get it all the time, but you have to let them know you're not here for your own health or they will slack any chance they get. It doesn't hurt to be a passive-aggressive trainer, either, unless it completely kills your communication skills as well. Clients need to talk. It is their time to get it out with someone they trust who is impartial (hopefully) or has good judgment and sound advice.

I train some very intelligent people, and although I am

damn good at my job and quite well rounded educationally, it would be a gross error to believe I am smarter than they are. The only edge I have is that when you are too close to something you cannot always see the forest through the trees.

Thankfully, I am also not prejudiced to the trivial circumstances of a particular situation and able to remain unattached emotionally to a desirable outcome, so I can shine the light on something if so inclined.

Nonetheless, if they press and I don't want to respond (even though it pisses them off sometimes), my trademark answer is "By remaining neutral, I am best able to observe and facilitate your progress."

This is why I mentioned the psychology reference from college earlier because that is what it all boils down to other than a kick-ass workout.

I spot-check the nearest bench press, and a butch-as-hell dude wearing black combat boots, cutoff camouflaged shorts, random tattoos, a peroxide Guy Fieri- styled haircut, and enough piercings to kill a small animal—not to mention he is hugely vascular and obviously 'roided out from his toes to his eyeballs—is talking to another guy, so I casually stroll over and ask politely, "How many sets do you have left?"

I hear him finish his sentence, "and add a teaspoon of coriander, Mikey," in a voice higher than Michael Jackson's. He turns and says, "I only have one more left," with bent wrists flailing as he animates his huge arms.

I have to regain my composure. "Umm, thanks."

Even Kris says, "That's just wrong. That's like walking up to pet a Labrador and it meows!" I have to laugh as I remember that this is one of those 250- to 300-pound muscularly ripped guys I see on Santa Monica Boulevard in Weho sometimes, walking their outfitted, tiny doggies on a leash.

We are halfway through when Kris is struggling to finish a tough set and he stops.

"What are you doing, that wasn't muscular failure. Why did you stop?"

He looks at me with a twisted face of confusion and pain.

"Are you okay?"

He stands up and walks away. I watch him utterly perplexed. He turns around and comes back, looks me in the eye, and as a single tear rolls down his face he says, "I can't train with you anymore."

"Whoa, where did that come from?"

"I couldn't tell you earlier. I have to go back east for a while. My father has cancer and my mother has Alzheimer's. Sometimes . . . sometimes she doesn't even know who I am." He almost breaks down again.

What can I do? Give him a hug? Other gawking gym rats and trainers are already scoping us. No, not in this gym, or next week it'll be rumored that I do full-service back scrubs in the shower too.

Fuck everybody else. I have genuine empathy for him. I put my hand on his shoulder while he sits with his hands in his face for a minute.

This guy is a very creative, successful designer for the highest echelon of people. He has clients in countries all over the world, but most importantly he makes me laugh all the time. That is what I Love about this guy, his sense of humor. He could have done stand-up. I mean this is the client who told me he wants his "calves so big that I can get small flat-screen TVs installed in the back of them like the car headrests on the show *Pimp My Ride!*" the first day I asked him his goals for his "chicken legs."

I struggle to find the words, "I'm so sorry, you never said anything."

"When I'm here with you, I sort of forget about all of it for an hour."

"When are you leaving?"

"Next month, but I wanted to let you know as soon as possible. I don't want to quit now that my body is changing. I was really in Palm Springs this weekend to sell my other house."

"I'm sorry."

"Thanks. It's all right. Let's finish this workout. I'll be here like normal 'til I leave. Not sure of the exact date yet."

"Okay. Let's do this." We blast through the rest, and I wonder how I would deal with the same distress and whether I will have to someday.

* * *

My manager is puckering up to someone. As I say goodbye to Kris, he walks straight up to me with this new member. The guy must be a baller, or he wouldn't get this much attention.

"I would like you to meet Shawn and give him a complimentary workout and stretch session. He is ready to go!"

I extend my hand for a proper introduction, "Hi, I'm Devon. Nice to meet you."

I look at my manager and use all my will to not give him *that* look. You know, the sour look, like you're sucking on a lemon.

"No, I don't mind, but I would like to get some sort of assessment of your fitness level, present or past injuries, spinal and health concerns, and whatnot, first."

"Oh, I'm as fit as a fiddle, boy," Shawn responds.

He looks like he just swallowed a bowling ball for breakfast, and he just called me "boy."

"Yeah, he will be fine, just give him an overall body

conditioning workout, thanks. Have a good workout Shawn."

That was coming from a manager who spews the words "safety," "knowledge," "expertise," and "professionalism" in one sentence. What a cheeseball!

As soon as he walks away, Shawn starts pride-pumping himself. I am curious to see if he is going to be one of those ole glory days kind of guys.

"I used to play football in high school. I was bulletproof back in the day, so how long will it take to lose this. Muscle has memory, don't it? I got three months before my weddin' and my doctor says I need to cut back on the salt a little bit. So, what do you think?"

Now, what would you do? He looks at least forty-five to fifty, so he took at least fifteen to twenty years to build that huge, obscene gut. Obviously, he has hypertension, and he thinks three months is going to be enough. Yeah, muscle has a response time if it has previously been conditioned but no, blockhead, only your mind has memory. That's why you have a brain—or not! *Only in LA?* No. This takes place all over the US with the baby boomers and people who think they can get in shape overnight. Maybe it's the fitness marketing ads that mislead them?

It turns out that Shawn is a huge commodities trader and oil well owner from Texas, and that he is going to buy out a local studio production department as a graduation present for his son, who is going to USC for film school. He says his son is going to make some "movin' pictures."

While Shawn was in LA, he happened to meet this pretty, little woman whom he fell in Love with and since he has been here in Tinseltown, he has come to the surprising realization that he is fat.

I tell him he can do it only if he follows exactly what I

tell him to do. Of course, he says "yes" and that he is "totally committed," but they all say that. "Actions speak louder than words," and "Only time will tell," are the perfect phrases to determine whether he is blowing smoke up my ass or whether he is a man of his word. If he can give up his whiskey cocktails, surf and turf dinners, and bottles of vino every night, then we have a deal. Otherwise, he can find some other trainer to kiss his ass and pussyfoot around the gym everyday while he eats five thousand calories a night and wastes my time.

Please keep in mind that he is a gym client and not a private, so I will not get any more monetary compensation from this one, than any other client here, plus I don't play favorites. I will respect his word and keep mine, but he has to earn it like everybody else. He can't buy his way out of it.

Must be nice to be his son though. "Hey Dad, I want to make films, but I need a film studio or something?" "Don't worry son I'll take care of it, you just have a good time taking one of the most expensive college curriculums in Southern California, alright." Just joking, but from my perspective, it is sort of mind-blowing, or mind-numbing, I am not sure which.

We are halfway through the warm-up and then it happens, "Oh, I forgot to tell you, I tore my shoulder a couple years ago working out with my brother doing incline presses."

"Glad you remembered to tell me that. It's important."

I am thinking that my manager is an incompetent farce and Shawn is a neglectful moron for completely ignoring what I said to them earlier like I was a school kid with no experience at all. "Well, that changes a few things. Have you rehabilitated it?"

"I stopped working out 'cause it hurt if that's what you mean?"

"No, I mean did you receive any therapy for your labrum or rotator cuff after the sports doctor diagnosed the tear?"

"I didn't see a doctor."

"So, you just stopped working out? How does it feel now?"

"Well, it bothers me a bit if I sleep on that side at night, or if I am carrying my briefcase all day."

"Okay, that's good news. It has healed but it is weak, and it gets inflamed when pressure causes it to sit in the shoulder socket in an unbalanced way."

"Umm, I guess so. What does that mean?"

"It means we need to condition the tendons and ligaments surrounding the joint and work on strengthening the rotator cuff muscles as well. Plus, work on your postural muscles."

"Well let's get to it, boy."

I lead the way. He is clueless. This is going to be a long one. Shawn is impatient, I can tell. He keeps pointing to a loudmouth, showboat trainer who is spotting this big guy like him. Shawn wants to lift heavy like that and be a manly man, but I won't let him. His shoulder is really weak, and I do not want to be responsible for him injuring it any further.

"When will I be able to do that again?" he points to the two doing incline presses.

"Never," I tell him.

He looks at me like I just took candy away from a baby. I tell Shawn that if he hurts himself at the start of his fitness endeavors then he will never reach his goals, and that the trainer he is watching isn't even making sure the guy has good form. He is still unhappy and not used to being corralled. This relationship won't last long.

When a client gets hurt using an incompetent "trainer", he/she loses confidence in the trainer and the new goals.

The momentum is killed off and so is their inspiration. Sometimes this is all it takes to prevent a person from getting back into shape forever.

We finish, and Shawn stubbornly admits, "I know you know what you're doing and I'm glad I'm with you, boy, I would have hurt myself again and been back to square one."

I tell him, "Well, don't put the cart before the horse, 'cause you have a ways to go."

He understands this term, and laughs and slaps me on the back, "See you Tuesday, boy."

Maybe I was wrong, there is hope. I just have to get used to the "boy" part.

* * *

Today is my last workout with Vikram. I tried to get used to his name but ended up calling him Vik. We have been tackling his Indian, body fat situation for about six months now and it is time for him to graduate from Pepperdine University and move on.

He is working on his thesis. I think Vikram's Master in Psychology is justified the same as everyone else who studies it. Basically, he is just trying to understand himself, and why he may or may not be messed up in his own mind.

He is very analytical and at least he doesn't talk about the same subject matter as most people in the entertainment industry, the cinephiles, and the rest of the newly transplanted that are also trying to figure themselves out too.

I am not one hundred percent sure, but I think he is a closeted homosexual who hasn't come to terms with it and cannot bring himself to because his father would come unglued. He would be at risk of losing all of his academic backing, not to mention his share of the estate, and his inheritance his father has promised him as long as he provides an heir.

Talk about pressure to perform. His only other siblings are sisters, so he is expected to go forth into that good night and conceive after he finds a wife of worthy acceptance. He also has to keep a four-point grade average all along the way, or his father will cut off his allowance too.

I cannot say I would switch places with him. I would at least want to figure things out just like he is so desperately trying to accomplish. It is going to take more than a PhD to bring his father's dream of Vikram running a practice and having a happy-go-lucky nuclear family nearby as well, to positive fruition.

I just make him warm up for twenty minutes to get to his fat burning mode and then put him through a forty-minute resistance machine circuit. It is a walk through the gym-park. He can't take any more than that before he starts to die on me anyway. His brain is so overtaxed, that his body only allows him to get away with so much. I do my best to stretch his inflexible limbs. Vik is toast so I let him go, sincerely wish him good luck, and watch him as he meanders out the two front doors to a Life in a vice mentality.

* * *

I leave the gym, and go up in the Hollywood hills to work with my other neophyte, Jason. When I get there, he is ready and looking much better than the day we met. He almost seems like a different person, and I am relieved to see some spunk in him. I tell him to put on his kicks and meet me outside.

He walks outside to the narrow road and we start to run. This is all we will do today, a simple jog. No fancy stuff. We are going back to the basics. As his health progresses, we will go to the beach, mountain bike, go swimming, surfing, rock-climbing, hiking, and whatever else blows his hair back. He is already skinny. He just needs a new high, a natural high.

He probably thought I was going to promptly pull out the weights on him and I will incorporate that, and kickboxing, into his regimen a couple times a week. Right now, all he needs is to just get his blood moving and experience the healing power of activity in nature. If he had this, he wouldn't have got caught up in that drug scene in the first place.

This guy is going to be all right. I can tell even though we have to stop every five minutes so he doesn't collapse right there on the road. We have to be aware of paparazzi as well. It is not my job to worry about that but why not? They would kill to get shots of him right now in his not so vibrant state bending over at the waist to catch his breath, or possibly throw up. His publicists wouldn't like that. He brought it on himself though, and they say no free press is bad press, but I am innately a little protective. The photographers have no ethics, so I make sure he wears a cap, sunglasses, stays off the main roads, and doesn't have to talk to anyone.

I make him stretch himself out by showing him the stretches and decide he's had enough.

"Good job, Jason. Next time eat some oatmeal an hour before we meet, put on sunscreen, and plan on being gone for three hours or more, cause we're going to the beach."

He says, and I quote, "Cool dude, late!"

* * *

I am waiting for the Guru Chick to poke me with sharp objects again. Needles used to make me queasy and pass out. Being stabbed by them so much in the Army got me used to it, I guess. I could draw my own blood now and not even flinch.

Peoples' pain thresholds are different though. They are

different in type and area as well. My friend, who is a martial arts nut, can break a baseball bat with his shin and take kicks to his thighs, which is a bruising sort of pain. I have seen him do it at public demonstrations with the World Tae Kwon Do team. If you go up to him and pinch him on the back of his arm, he squeals like a baby pig though. Similarly, when I am training some people, they will get nauseous doing biceps and some doing legs. It is all relative to the pain stimulus and their neurological tolerance.

I sit in the lobby waiting for my turn. She greets me with her ceremonial white robe and head turban on. She is full of smiles and always gives me a hug and asks how I am feeling. I tell her I am doing well compared to most, but I feel like something is missing. She tells me to lie down, be still, and breathe. Then she puts her hands over me and stands there like that for a minute or more with her eyes closed.

She says, "You have lost the fun. You need to find something you like to do again and do it."

"I am trying."

"No, you don't know what it is right now because you have not let go of your pain enough to let it in."

"Let what in?"

"Exactly."

It takes me a second to get this. "Ohhhh, okay. You mean how can I know because I am not leaving room for anything to enter my Life?"

She smiles and says, "When you can let go, new things will come into your Life because there will be room for a transitional shift, but you must realize that this shift is not tangible. It is a shift in consciousness."

She loses me again.

She sees my bewildered face, pauses, and puts her hand on my forehead and whispers, "Meditate on it."

This seems like a throwaway. It reminds me of the same response I used to get as a kid, "Pray about it." Meditate on it/Pray about it, they mean the same thing to me. "Okay, I will, thanks." What else can you say?

"Have you been taking your herbs?"

"Umm, a little."

"You need to do better."

I feel like the shoe is on the other foot. This must be how my clients feel when I question them about their diets and whether they are taking their supplements.

She looks at my tongue and almost winces. Then she tells me to save my energy and rest because she is going to do a special treatment with a lot of needles.

I thought I was pretty healthy, but it turns out my yin is not equal to my yang. Yeah, whatever. Yang this. So, I do what she says and start to doze off to never-never land.

* * *

I leave my appointment with Miss Guru Chick, and in my peaceful Zen-like state, I can now handle my next hour — or I should say hour and a half — with Amanda. She takes all my strength to be patient with. It takes more energy to listen intently than to talk. This is a fact.

I drive up her gated driveway in East Bel Air and she is still wearing a robe. She hasn't even gotten dressed today, much less warmed up like she is supposed to do before I get there. I go into the library and read or watch TV until the maid comes and gets me to let me know that her highness is ready for me now. The diva has absolutely no concept of time. It must be nice.

I walk into her workout room, or "studio" as she calls it. I helped her design it. No, not the decor, just the machines, equipment, and layout. She doesn't use half the stuff unless I force her to do it, but she had to have the whole shebang.

She is in a pink Juicy Couture sweat suit on the elliptical with her dog, Pooky, on the treadmill next to her, walking. If I didn't see it with my own eyes, I wouldn't believe it. She says Pooky's trainer taught her that! I wonder if he gets paid more than me. Maybe I need to switch vocations. She says it gets rid of her aggressive behavior towards other dogs. Can you believe it? *Only in LA.*

"So how do I look? I am doing the master cleanse right now. Do you think it is working?"

"Your skin looks great, Amanda."

"Do you think so. Thanks, you're so sweet . . . You just made my day. Really? Maybe I will go to that party tonight. Do you think I should? But then I have that meeting at two tomorrow with that director and producer. I look fabulous, huh. It's working but I am really cranky sometimes. And I crave the most crazy things. Let me tell you, I almost blew it last night. I was at Sweet Lady Jane's on Melrose to pick out Sara's birthday cake for next week and OH MY GOD! It smelled so good in there, and they offered me chocolate cake to sample along with the other kinds they had in the store or that they can make, and Devon, Devon . . . I almost ate it! I didn't though, I was a GOOD GIRL. Aren't you proud of me?

After this I am going to go on a new diet. Either South Beach or that one where you don't mix the types, or what about that blood type one—didn't you say that was bullshit—I don't know. YES, I DO! I want to go vegan again, so you have to make a menu plan again for me. Except this time, I need one for each day of the week and talk to the chef, too, because I want you to tell him about trans fats and the sodium stuff, and the right type of soy products to buy for me because you're better at explaining that stuff. I get confused, anyway. Do you really think my skin looks good?!"

She can go on like this for days if I just keep my mouth shut. Sometimes I just tune her out and am there for nothing more than morale support while she almost breaks a sweat. She often tells me she shouldn't sweat because "That's nasty, ladies don't sweat," and "It will mess up my do." And you wonder why her husband is never home. I Love her, but she takes some getting used to. I usually say, "To Love Amanda, is to know Amanda," or is it "To know Amanda, is to Love Amanda?" I don't know. Anyway, I have to interrupt her, or our time together will never end, and I will be there all day.

* * *

Next, I head out to Sammy's in Malibu. He usually works out early mornings, as do most professionals or businesspeople.

Depending on whether a person is an early riser or nocturnal is how to determine when it is best to work out for optimal results and/or intensity. Most people with families or limited income across America do not have the luxury of choosing.

Generally speaking, people who work out midday tend to be slightly flakier and are often not as on time either. That is why training movie stars, musicians, models, and creative people who have their own businesses can be way overrated.

Yeah, they are cool, and fun, and if you are a "name dropper", then you can pat your happy ass on the back for having them. If you are mutually respected or "cool" then maybe you'll get to hang with them, and if that is the wind beneath your wings then that will go a little ways as well, but the truth is while you are "hangin' out" you are not making any money, so big deal.

They also rarely refer other clients if you're that good and well-liked because they sort of (even if it is subconscious) want to keep you to themselves for whatever reason (i.e., control, scheduling freedom, exclusivity, etc.). If you aren't that good, and you cling on to them in any way, then you are stupid because they will sense it and you will be like all the other people who have no sense of identity, or individuality, and they will either categorize you with other commoners who foam at the mouth with admiration, or think you are after their cash just like everyone else who provides some kind of service.

The ocean is majestic, even in the twilight as I speed up to 110 on my bike on PCH. (Pacific Coast Highway). I feel alive as I blow past a few cars to go up the canyon to his estate. The house looks like it has been uprooted from the South and brought here as a transplant with its big white columns and huge front steps to the double doors.

I downshift and park out front. I can do that. Most people have to park in the designated visitor section after being let in by a personal guard at the long, sweeping iron gates below. I take my shiny, multicolored Aria helmet and my leather riding-jacket off, take one more look at the disappearing beautiful view of pink and orange clouds hovering over the water and being swallowed up by the dusk, and go in the side door to the house where the gym is located.

As I walk inside, Sammy is already warming up just like clockwork.

"Hey, how are you?"

He gives me a look of stress but smiles and says, "I am good, how are you?"

"Pretty good. Can't complain."

"Thank you for coming out on such short notice, but I will not be able to work out the rest of the week. I have to go out of town, so we will resume training on Monday morning like usual."

"No problemo."

"Great, now are you going to finally give me a real workout or do I have to look for a new trainer?"

"Are you going to start finally working out hard or should I find you a sweeter-tempered, gentler trainer?"

We both laugh. I kill this guy, and he Loves it and asks for more, so much fun.

"I want to invite you to my daughter's wedding, but you have to wear a suit. Do you have one?"

"A suit? What's that?"

He deadpans, "You are always so serious. How do you live this way? Oh, before I forget, she wants you to help her lose at least five pounds before her special day, so I am gonna make you an offer you can't refuse."

"Again, no problemo!"

"That's the right answer! She wants to start tomorrow, now let's get going, I don't have all day. I have dinner plans with my family."

"Well if you would stop talking then maybe we could start. C'mon soldier, your movin' like pond water!"

He pantomimes giving me a backhand across my face then he smiles, all in good fun.

In the middle of the workout, he intensely walks up to the television set. He then proceeds to call the person on the news broadcast a "schmuck," or a "bitch," especially when they put up two different political, opinionated parties to debate some recent happening or relevant issue. I just laugh because we both know they are full of it and just stirring the soup, but he gets so passionate about it.

It is the end, and even though he is exhausted and sweating like a whore in church, he says, "Finally, finally you give me a gooda workout, Grazie!"

"Finally, you do a gooda job"

He laughs, "Now go before my wife divorces me for missing dinner. See you Monday. Have a good weekend and stay out of a trouble."

"You, too."

* * *

"C'mon Linda, five more kicks, you can do it! Five, four, three, two, one, kick-ass! Now one more of each." The phone rings again.

"Fuck! Give me that damn thing!" She takes it and looks at the caller ID.

"It's my secretary. Talk to me. No shit? Uh-huh. No, fuck him! I told him he could use the jet only for the Comic-Con convention with Keanu and Vin Diesel. He can walk for all I care right now. If he doesn't get on that plane, I will sue his ass for breach of contract. Let him know he is obligated, and that I don't care if he has to share, that's too damn bad!" She hands me back the phone. "Fucking movie stars. People are starving in Africa and they are worried about their bullshit perks and accommodating their fucking entourage!"

"Wow . . ." That's all I can say at the moment.

Yes, I have had a client or two fly me somewhere for a little vacation/ training sojourn, but this kind of overblown, egomaniac stuff still boggles my mind. I hate it when I hear firsthand how someone who was a nobody here has, in the span of five years, become a self-centered, pompous prick.

These tyro celebs are usually the same ones who create a nihilistic society by doggin' out the federal government on TV, but at the same time are not doing anything positive to bring about change for the better. Anyone can point a finger and have an opinion, but why aren't you using your stardom to influence others proactively for the very thing you are bitching about?

It is not all of them, just a few bad apples who think they know everything, can't keep their mouth shut, and start to believe in the illusion of Hollywood and they're statuesque fame. For the record though, I must give props to the ones who are borderline philanthropists, and to those who do quite a great deal of charity work for diseases and such.

"Do you want to go to the premiere?" Linda asks.

"Yeah, sure, if it's not a pain in the—"

"Shut up, just call Kim and tell her I said to leave two tickets at will call."

"Thanks, will do. Now do five more."

"But you said—"

"Have you ever been lied to before?"

She nods her head, yes.

"Then you'll get over it."

"You suck, do you still want those tickets or not?"

"Won't work."

"Did I say you suck. I'm not happy about this exercise right now."

"Oh boohoo, poor Linda. Here let me wipe that sweat off your brow, or is that a tear?" I lift the towel to her forehead. She pushes my hand away.

"Fuck you," she growls.

"Now that's not very ladylike."

"You will like this movie a lot. It's good."

"It must be, I've never heard you say that before. You always say they suck."

She is panting but still trying to talk. I find it somewhat amusing.

"Not this one. Oscar potential."

"Really?"

"Yeah, I'll be busy, but If you see me, come and say hello."

"I really don't want to bother you, I—"

"Shut UP! Just do it!"

"Yes, Ma'am!"

"Don't call me that, it makes me feel old."

"Yes, Ma'am."

"Fuck you," She says exhausted as she collapses on the floor. "I'm toast, go home, see you tomorrow, goodbye."

"You have one more—"

"NO!"

"Calm down, just joking, let's stretch."

"Thanks, you know that's my favorite part, but I can't, have to go. See you tomorrow, have a good time. The party will be fun!"

"Okay, bye. Good job today, that was a good one."

"Thanks."

* * *

Airport traffic sucks. I have been summoned to pick up Cin and see her off. Happy, happy, joy, joy.

I pull up to the front with the Jeep, grit my teeth, and try to hold on to my pleasant edge a little before her presence all but wipes it away.

Somehow, when you see her in person, you forget all that anyway because she is so friggin' cute and sweet in a major girly way. Like she is a helpless stray lamb who has lost its way. Half of it has got to be an act but guys fall for it almost every time.

The girl is late. Wow, big surprise. She was probably even born late. She pops her head out the door with nothing.

"Let's go!" I yell.

Of course, she over packed, and I am the mule to bear the load. Upon finally getting everything in the car, she realizes she forgot something and has to go back inside. This cannot end too soon. She gets in and starts straight away.

"Why are guys so shitty?"

"What!"

"Why are guys so mean to me?"

"Listen, don't say that to the one guy who is helping you out right now or you'll be going to the airport in a taxi!"

"No, I don't mean you silly, you don't count."

"Oh, so now I don't count? I'm not a guy?"

"You know what I mean. You aren't like that. Why can't guys be more like you, I'm cursed, it must be pheromones, or something?"

"Cindy, did you ever stop to realize that you let guys shit on you, and the fact that you are attracted to bad-boy assholes, is an open invitation for a guy to take advantage of this?"

"I don't—"

"Stop. Just stop. You know that's true so don't even say it."

"D," she pouts.

"No offense, but don't you think it has something to do with your dad?"

"No, I went to therapy for a couple months, and my mom and dad just had their thirtieth wedding anniversary."

"So what! A couple months is a drop in the bucket, and that doesn't prove you weren't programmed differently, or that your parents did a good job with you. Somehow, someway, you need to change, or you will always have this problem. That's all I'm gonna say, end of discussion, change the topic."

"D," she says again with a pouty smile.

"Just think about it, hell, pray about it while you're gone, and in time it will make sense to you."

Silence, blissful silence, for at least a minute.

"Okay D, you're right, I will. Now do you want me to bring you back a cute T-shirt?"

In one ear and out the other, did it even land anywhere? I am left to wonder if any of that had any cerebral impaction at all.

THE PREMIERE

MAY 13

I just dumped Cin off and I am cruising back. It is sunny. I am free to be me for the rest of the day, and I am happy. I am excited to go to the movie premiere tonight.

The phone rings and it is Jay. I answer.

"What up?"

"Hey, what you gettin' into tonight, dog, I have a few honeys coming by the restaurant and we are going to the clubs afterward, so I'll pick you up about eight or so, a'ight, peace."

"Wait, wait, hold up, damn. I am going to a premiere tonight."

"What? With whom? C'mon now, hook a Brotha' up!"

"Oh, do you want to go? Maybe we can hold hands on the red carpet?"

"Well now, fuck you too buddy," he says in his ultra "whiteboy" tone.

"Well . . ."

"A'ight you got me, have a good time dog, and call me when you leave 'cause we will still be kickin' it."

"Roger that, out."

He wants to be an actor, or I should say, a known name,

working actor. He will hold it against me that I am not taking him, whether he says so or not.

Everyone wants to go to the premieres. After a while, they are all the same, but you have to be seen and mingle with as many industry people to be in the game in this town or you will go nowhere.

It is six already. They never start on time, which is always seven thirty, but I like to be early to run into a few acquaintances. Helps me relax and feel comfortable in my surroundings.

These things tend to have that electric feeling in the air. When I am going to something to have a good time and put out that positive vibe, I hate to rush. It just crushes the smoothness and people can feel it. I have met the coolest actors and people who worked on the film when I am laid back, have no expectations, and am just happy to be there. It is that idea of when you look for something is when you never find it, and when you don't, it just pops up in your face. Gotta take a shower.

I stop by the Hard Rock and have a drink before the show. There is already a media craze and spectator madness going on. The event is at Universal, so the crowds tend to be enormous.

I start to walk onto the red carpet, but I hesitate and slow down so I can follow three dressed up hotties. I figure if I am going to be frivolously outshined because I am not famous then I might as well enjoy the view along the way. The carpet started way further back this time because there is a stage where they are playing music and interviewing the key players for the movie. Linda wasn't lying; this is a big one.

I catch up to the girls when we enter the amphitheater, and they smile and say hello. I walk up to grab a complimentary popcorn and diet coke, and hand them each one. We chat for a bit, but they are on full star-watch alert and acting like they are at prom, so I quickly excuse myself and head for my seat.

Wow, she hooked me up! I am sitting in the lowest section right in front of Hillary Duff. In your face shorty!

I feel guilty that the seat next to me is empty though. What a waste. I tried to ask a few girls, but they were too stuck-up to come, I guess. Sad, just sad, any girl standing along the velvet ropes on the way in would have jumped at the chance to have a little fun. Girls these days, I just don't get them. Either that, or it is because I practically have "Damaged Goods" written on my forehead.

So, I watch the celebs come in and get interviewed on the screen in front, eat my snack, and wait for them to usher everyone in from the lobby by threatening the start of the movie. The lights go dim. The VIPs are still walking to their seats.

The energy is always positive at a premiere because the studio people, their family, and friends are all gunning for the movie, so it is a different vibe than if you saw it on the weekend at the Cineplex. Everyone yells, whistles, and claps during the credits as it starts like a school basketball rally.

* * *

It was good. A tearjerker like I have not seen in a while, hardly a dry eye in the house. The after party is in the New York section of the studio, so we have to walk like a herd of cows to the spot with tickets in hand for the ushers to check along the way. Not everyone who goes to the movie gets to go to the after party.

We reach it and it is movie themed. There are a few games and music being sung by a gospel choir from the movie. The air is filled with the smell of food, and I immediately get in line to eat. I grab some grub and head for the nearest table.

My attention is focused solely on my plate as small groups of people come over and sit down, and the area becomes swollen with bodies. Everyone is cool to me, but I take a pause from my consumption and look around and realize that I am sitting smack dab in the middle of a reserved section of names. Some are familiar and some completely elude me. Nonetheless, I trudge forward stuffing my mouth with food until I am blindsided by her presence, and almost choke on my salad.

She is standing at a small bar table and elegantly sipping white wine. It is Calista. The dress she wears makes her impossible to ignore, and she is the center of attention for anyone who is in eyesight. She looks perfect, and could be, too, unless I am putting her so high on a pedestal that I am blinded by my own naïve perception. It could be a blessing or a curse.

I have to stop eating because I am so instantly intrigued and cautious at the same time. "Cautious," how pathetic. Calista is my new muse, Queen of "Liberation," a cherished soul-saver . . . or breaker?

She sets down her glass and starts to walk toward me. I am about to panic. Maybe I should have brought my friend Jay, the crutch who pads the awkwardness and always smooths things over.

I wipe my mouth off and start to stand up as she glides right past me as if I am invisible. From behind, I hear Linda's voice and I do a one-eighty. As I swivel around, Linda looks right at me and I start to turn back in embarrassment.

"Devon!"

I turn back around not knowing what to do.

"Devon, I want you to meet someone. This is Richard,

our president of production, and this is Stephanie, our vice president of production."

"Hi, nice to meet you." I shake their hands and imply as much respect as possible.

"Devon is the one who kicks my ass every day." They all give her a courtesy chuckle as we are softly interrupted.

I hear Linda say, "Oh, hello, beautiful. How are you?" as she gives Calista a hug right next to me.

I want to be inconspicuous, but try as I might, I can't help but fixedly stare. Linda sees this. I must look like a bashful little boy.

"Calista, I would like you to meet Devon."

"Hi, how are you? You look familiar, I think we have met before."

She does remember me. Linda responds.

"Devon, you do really get around don't you, you little devil."

I am blushing at maximum capacity now. Calista makes the connection.

"Yeah, we met at that restaurant on Melrose."

I guess it is my turn, I should say something.

"Yeah, now I remember, you were celebrating your birthday."

Linda gives me a wink and starts to pull her entourage away by the arms, and it dawns on me why she is the great facilitator that she is in this business as I have just witnessed it firsthand.

"I have to make the rounds so I will leave you in very capable hands Calista, and I will see you tomorrow, Devon, enjoy."

Linda is da bomb; I am going to give her a back massage and a full, stretching session if I survive this.

Calista comes a little closer and I can smell her scent, or

at least the shampoo she used last. I don't care, it's all good. I am at the gates of heaven, but will she let me in?

"You're a cute one. And to think I let you get away. What do you do, how do you know Linda?"

Here it comes, the basic bullshit cue of the traditional status report. This is when I crumble to the onslaught of insecurity. So, of course I overcompensate.

I give her my best seductive look and cheesily say, "It's not what I do, it's what I'm gonna do to you . . ."

She laughs, that's a good sign. How much longer can I front.

"Yes, of course, now it is all clear, Mr. Anytime. What makes you think you have what it takes?"

Damn, she is a feisty one. It works better this way though. At least I can fight the good fight when the ball is served back to my side of the court.

"There is only one way to find out, Princess."

"Hhmm . . . All right I'll bite, give me your number and I'll give you a ring when I can find some time to have a nice, quiet lunch, or a very discreet dinner excursion."

I reach in my pocket promptly for I am always ready to give out my digital QR business card.

"I give great massages, too."

She sticks the card in her purse, grins seductively, and floats away. I am in a trance. I am full of anxiety and supposition. Will she really call? It is truly an unbelievable moment, and I can only smile and enjoy it because who knows if I will ever have another one like this. *Only in LA.*

I look around and notice that the movie premiere and the gym crowds are two correlative entities. Except here, they are dressed up, more full of it, and buzzed. I stick around the circus a while to mix it up with the posers, the lushes who can't help themselves, and the ladies of the evening.

While I mingle, I get my entertainment by observing the declarations of lie and deceit which always sound like, "That was the best movie I have ever seen," "Those special effects were breathtaking," or "That scene was just genius," and "Her acting was amazing, Oscar caliber all the way." These cheesy, ass- kissing remarks I overhear are when I almost blow my drink through my nose to keep from laughing.

Then you have the people who work there, who either can't be bothered by the whole scene and keep looking at their watches so they can escape the humdrum monotony, or the marketing assistants-turned-ushers who think their job is a matter of national security.

After a while, it gets sad, so I leave to turn in. Have to be up early again to be Mr. Jones' inspiration tomorrow. Oh shit, I am going to get only three hours of sleep. Tomorrow will be like being a vampire on a day pass. Great! I'll just think about Calista all day. It will pull me through.

THE DAY AFTER

MAY 14

Mr. Jones is sweating his ass off this morning.

"I am so bloody thirsty, and I feel so bloated," he says in his thick British accent.

"What did you eat yesterday?"

"I had dinner at a restaurant, and I ordered soup, salad, pasta, and veal."

"Was it salty food and did you have drinks?"

"I had a cocktail and a glass and a half of wine, come to think of it, it was quite salty, I remember commenting to my wife that very thing."

"That's why you're sweaty and dehydrated. Just keep drinking water all day and it will filter out by this afternoon and take some Uva-Ursi herb. Restaurants try to make the food taste better by dumping on the sodium, but it is hard on the body that way. Plus, you had carbs which hold water and alcohol, which displaces water, so no wonder you feel that way."

"Good to know, good to know. Thank you."

"Don't mention it."

Us trainers are full of these tidbits of knowledge. I held back so as not to overwhelm him with stuff. Just a small amount at a time, or none of it will be retained. Mr. Jones comes to the gym every morning, so he didn't hire me for discipline like most people. He hired me to be pushed, for proper biomechanics (form), and knowledge. This is what I like.

He is afraid to do the next set, I can tell.

"C'mon, you can do it, I'm here, I'll spot you, I wouldn't ask you to do anything I didn't have one hundred percent faith in, do it for the Queen, it will be easy."

"Yeah, EASY for you to say!"

He does it, and I give him a high five as he has just achieved a new goal.

I tell him, "If you accomplish nothing else today, you can be rest assured that you have reached a new 'benchmark' in your healthy challenge of choice before most people even get out of bed. Now that's a trooper!"

He just smiles nonchalantly and says, "Thank you, my dear friend."

"You're welcome!"

Can anyone say too much caffeine?

"What are you doing this evening, Devon?"

"I have to train a client at seven, in a high-rise off Wilshire."

"Come by the store after and watch the fashion show. Have a martini on us. We are launching a new men's sportswear line and a new women's line as well, so it will be a good mixed crowd. You will have a smashing time, I'm sure."

"I'll be there after I train Vincent."

"If he has not already been formally invited let him know he can come along."

"Will do. Now let's do this set!"

"Bullocks, I was hoping you'd forgotten the last one, and I could go now."

"Nope, one more for the road."

"You're a killer."

* * *

Shawn walks in, and he looks like shit. He has brought his new significant other with him. She is wearing Ugg boots, a stocking cap, big, black-framed sunglasses, a crop top, camouflage stretch jeans, and has not stopped talking on her cell phone since she walked in the door. Now, she is on the Stairmaster barely moving like this. *Only in LA.*

He perks up as he introduces me although she says, "Hi," and just keeps on spewing out her phone drama. I'm not saying she's a gold digger, but the thought did cross my mind, and something seems amiss. On one scale though, they are perfect for each other, cluelessly annoying, on their own planet, and everything else revolves around them.

"I just want to be stretched today."

Great, just what I want to do is break a sweat stretching his big ass. Lifting this behemoth's legs with tight as hell hamstrings could almost give me a hernia.

"What's up? Getting lazy on me?"

"No, I have to go back to Texas today. I have been up all night. Not a wink. My company is being accused of insider trading and I have to go put out the fire. I don't know how long I will be gone, and she might go with me."

"I am surprised you even showed up."

"I thought it might help my stress level."

"Really? Wow! You're in danger of becoming a bona fide gym rat."

"Yeah, yeah, yeah, bust my balls some more while you're at it. Get your shots in now 'cause this may be it."

"Let's go, just don't fall asleep on me."

* * *

I pick Jason up and we cruise to the beach. It is a bright

eighty-five and not a cloud in the sky. Jason is quiet, so I break the ice.

"Did you hear what Trump said when a reporter asked him how he felt about Roe versus Wade?"

He just shakes his head, no.

"He said, I don't give a damn how people get away from Hurricane Dorian as long as they leave!"

It takes almost a minute then he busts up.

"So did you do anything fun this weekend?"

"I just chilled. I am up for this part, and I am seeing a new girl I met."

"Oh so, that's what you're thinking about. What's she like?"

"She is like no one I have ever met, totally real. No star-struck bullshit. She just gets me, dude."

"Good for you. Sounds like a keeper. Anyone I know?"

"Yeah, that's the funny part. She's a name, but you would never expect her to be so cool. She went through the same crap I am going through now when she was a teenager growing up in this town, so she knows how to deal."

"What part?"

"Huh? Oh, it's this brother picture, and I am the younger one who has to bail out my brother from a prison camp in World War Two. If I get it, I will have to be on set for four months and in the Pacific Islands."

"Wow, party central dude!"

"Yeah, right."

"Actually, it would be good to get away, don't you think?"

"I don't know, I am kinda liking this girl, and chillin' with you. Everyone else is so fake."

"Yeah, well it's just the world we live in. So, are you ready? Let's do this!"

I finish parking on the side of PCH and get out. I open the back and grab two surfboards and look at Jason's reaction.

"We are going surfing?" he asks with reluctant surprise.

"I figured as much as you say 'dude', you should know how to surf, plus when you do get this movie, you should have this girl fly out and take her surfing with you. It will be the chance of a lifetime."

"How did you know she surfs?"

"I didn't."

"She will be so stoked! She has been wanting me to learn but . . ."

"But what?"

"I'm . . . I'm sort of afraid."

"Of what?"

He looks sheepishly away from me towards the water.

"Sharks . . ."

"What? Give me a break. You have a better chance getting struck by lightning! Don't be a pussy. You are going to have so much fun, you'll laugh at what you just said later. C'mon, grab a board, just do it. You'll thank me later."

He hesitates.

"I said let's go!"

We head down to the water with the gear and do the damn thing. It is a triumph. Jason is a born surfer and he didn't even know it. Him being a skateboarder definitely helped. After that, we go to have Thai at a hole-in-the-wall place that rocks. It is one of the best days I can remember in Southern Cali.

I drop him off, and I tell him next time we will meet at the gym to do some upper body conditioning because his legs will be sore tomorrow.

He replies, and I quote, "Cool, dude, thanks!"

* * *

Vincent cancels. He says he is sick. I get a call from Ryan, a long-lost client who has just got back into town, and on my way back through Beverly Hills, I stop by to train him.

Ryan is an entertainment lawyer who deciphers all that small text when an actor, or a musician, needs protection from getting screwed over by all the other word-beaters.

Here is another guy who has all this money, famous clients, dates a new woman every week, goes to all the posh places to be seen, hits all the coolest parties bicoastally (Miami to NYC), vacations at exotic locales all over the world (with a phone stuck to his ear), and is still not happy.

His world is spinning so fast all the time that he is in constant sensory overload. The sensationalism is so extreme that he has become numb from it. All he can do is go bigger, faster, and more, more, more, hoping to find something that is already there. He has everything, so what else is there? Can you say, "Taken for granted," or "Needs spiritual fulfillment?"

I couldn't even help this guy six months ago. I thought he was what successful men might aspire to be at one point until it all happened. I was blinded more than I even imagined by all the glitter and greed of what was hardly gold but a big lesson.

If God—the collective consciousness of the universe; the ultimate Creator; the infinite Spirit; your higher power; or whatever floats your boat to call It —has a sense of humor, then the joke was seriously on me. I have found the light and fortunately at the end of that cold, dark tunnel it was not another oncoming train.

The illusion of pride is humility, which will come. Have you received a wake-up call yet yourself? I hope you figure things out before it comes because when it does, brothers and sisters, be prepared for a little suffering and repentance. Hey, you know that saying, "Nothing in Life is free?" Well, there is a lot of truth to it. Truth.

The Discovery
and the Accident

May 22

It all started one morning. A morning like any other morning, I suppose. At this point in my Life, on a dawn like this, I would have used the expression "same shit, different day" in my same melancholic tone. I remember it so vibrantly clear that it seems like yesterday.

After flying down the highway at almost light speed at 4:45 in the morning, I pull up to Sammy's front gate and enter the gate code wondering where the guard is. Maybe he is just taking a piss? It opens, and I cruise up to where I normally park my bike. I get off, take off my gear, and go inside.

I walk in, mentally ready to reign, and am surprised to find Sammy not warming up. Surely someone should have informed me of his absence if he couldn't make it. Damn secretaries, I hate it when this happens. Quite irritated, I walk back outside to my bike.

I momentarily gaze at the sun beginning to peek over the horizon as I start to put on my jacket when I see a slight movement with my peripheral vision. I can't make it out at first until I realize there is a blood trail leading to it from outside of the parked Bentley. I run over to it without thinking.

It is Sammy. He is barely breathing and bleeding profusely.

"Sammy? Sammy, oh shit!"

He has been obviously beaten and shot as well. I pull out my cell and dial 911.

Sammy tries to speak, "Go help my family . . ."

His words are barely audible as blood starts to drain from the corner of his mouth.

"I'm not leaving you."

Then Sammy says it in a way I understood. "Fuck you, go find my kids."

I take off my T-shirt and start to apply a pressure tourniquet to his bleeding chest. "Hold this, I'll be right back."

Before I can even start to panic, I go to the cracked front door, sprint upstairs, and all I see to my horror, are bodies and blood in every room.

This is a family to me too. They invited me over for Thanksgiving and Christmas for God's sake.

I find them all, one by one, slumped over lying still like mannequins in a war zone. The last room I go into is the master bathroom, and I find his wife, Isabelle.

I can barely stand to look at her. She is naked in a satin robe and looks badly beat-up. I cover her body with a towel and leave.

I run out the front door hesitatingly because I'm not sure what to tell Sammy. I would never lie to him, but I don't want to kill him off with such a meager prognosis of his loved ones. I reach him and he is hardly breathing.

"You have to—"

"Don't speak," I say to him. "Save your strength."

I start to check his vital signs and place pressure on the wound.

"Help is on the way, just hang in there Sammy!"

"It was the—" His words are swallowed up by the gurgling blood rising from his internal bleeding.

"Shut up, tell me later."

I feel his presence going. "Don't leave me Sammy . . . Sammy!" I scream at him as I shake him like a 220-pound rag doll.

"Fuck this, this is not happening," I say to myself as I eye the keys on the ground to the car, he was so desperately trying to crawl back from, and fight the impulse to take him to the emergency room my damn self.

Even in this state, when everything seemed to be in slow motion, freeze frame I couldn't help but wonder why he was trying to get to his car in the first place.

Then at that moment, I hear the ambulance coming up the canyon. Sammy reaches in his pocket and hands me a manila envelope before he passes out. The ambulance drives up as I instinctively put the envelope in my cargo pocket, not really thinking as to why he would do such a thing, or what it is that he is really giving me.

I am now in shock and just stand there vapid, and stare at the paramedics as they begin to do what they do best. I look at the blood on my hands in dismay and disbelief. I feel weak, and slowly walk over to the front doorsteps almost at a stagger. I sit down and wait for the oncoming cavalry to arrive. I can now hear more sirens wailing in the background. It is going to be a long, long day.

* * *

My head is still spinning. The cops must have asked me a million questions. I ride to the gym in a daze. I don't know what to do, what to think, or feel. I just know that I can't train like this right now. Sammy was like a surrogate father-figure to me, whom I respected, and now he was gone.

He didn't make it. They lost him before he even got to Cedars Sinai. They should have sent for a Medevac helicopter, dammit. My heart feels more shattered than before. That seems impossible though. There is only an empty cavern of mashed humility left inside. I try to shrug it off as God's will.

I walk into my workplace and go directly to my manager's office.

"Do you have a minute?" I ask him completely monotone.

"Where have you been? You missed the training meeting. It was mandatory, remember? Or are you too cool to be reprimanded?"

I am blindsided by this.

"I'm sorry I was unable to make it because —"

"You think you can do whatever you want? How does that make me look? I'm trying to do a job here!"

"Whoa, please slow down a bit, I just had a client die and—"

"Couldn't have been a client from here, and if it wasn't then I don't want to hear it!"

"Look, I'm not dealing with this very well right now, so I came here to ask you—"

He turns his back on me as if to completely dismiss my concerns.

"I have to take a few days off."

"Oh, that's all? No problem. Go ahead, take as many as you want, but don't come back because there will be no work waiting for you."

"What? I've busted my ass for this place for five years!"

"Go cry on someone else's shoulder."

I would normally rip this guy's head off, but I can't bring myself to with the aftermath of violence I have witnessed today.

"Fuck you. You're a piece of shit, you know that!"

I storm out and slam his door as hard as I can. He yells but his voice is muffled by the door and walls that he hides behind.

I go outside and pace. I need a drink. I need something to escape this day. I ride to the Palm Restaurant on Santa Monica Boulevard and walk into the bar and order a Cutty Sark on the rocks. This is Sammy's favorite.

I raise the glass and say, "To you, Sammy."

I lower my head and force myself not to cry. Sammy wouldn't like that. He would smack me one right upside the face if I shed a tear over him.

It really isn't for him that I start to get weepy. It is the thought of his kids and Isabelle that keeps haunting me. I can't seem to get those images from the morning out of my head. They are on rapid replay.

I order another and slam it. My cell starts to ring. I see the number. It's her. She must be horny. Haven't seen her in a while because I told her I had to stop. Didn't feel right about it. I answer it anyway.

"What's up, beautiful, how are you doing?"

"I want you now. When can you come over?"

These Hollywood housewives—

"How about this evening, or better yet tomorrow? I'm just not—"

"No. Sooner!"

They can be so sexually demanding.

"Okay, I'll be right over."

"I miss you and I want you inside me."

She hangs up. I pay the man and exit.

* * *

All right, I never thought I would stoop to this level again, but her so-called man is evidently not taking care of business at home when this gorgeous woman is scheduling me in her daily routine for a booty call. It's a shitty job but somebody has to save her from a Life of pampered despair.

Maybe it will help me forget mine. This has to be up there with one of the worst days in LA so here I go, buzzed, off to fulfill her every sensual need. Hey, romance is dead anyway, didn't you know? Good sex is in.

I pull into the driveway, never knowing what to expect. She opens the door in her next-to-nothing nightgown. I pause with a hesitant look around for a potential husband's vehicle in the garage.

"He is in New York for two more days. The maids are off today. C'mon, I've been thinking about this all day!"

She pulls me upstairs to the bedroom, tearing my clothes off as we go. She likes it rough, so I slap her on the ass every now and then, and I don't hold back when I hold her tight in my muscle-bound grasp around her neck and waist while pounding her from behind. This is how she likes it.

She moans loudly as she reaches orgasm. It is her first, but this woman likes to have everything come in threes, as it so often does for her: three cars; three huge diamond rings; the three big shopping sprees a month at the three big stores on Wilshire Boulevard (Neiman's, Barney's, and Sak's, for those of you who don't know); three yearly exotic vacations, well you get the picture. So, I continue to rise to the occasion. If I don't? Well, she probably has three of us too. *Only in LA.*

* * *

I ride away exhausted but totally relaxed pondering, as it is against my ethical standards to sleep with a married woman, will my karma somehow be challenged by these promiscuous charades later on if I ever fall in Love again, and possibly tie the knot? I should be paying more attention. Yep, sometimes when you ask the universe a question you get an answer quicker than expected.

A truck with landscaping equipment blows out a tire right in front of me and starts to fishtail. Shit! I am going to be forced off the road. I gun it hoping to jump the rocks and crash onto the white sand of the beach below. Hey, it's softer than hitting the two cars in front of me that were skidding sideways.

If it were not so dark out now, I don't think I would have had the cojones to opt for the oceanic maneuver because I can't quite see how far, or exactly what I am going to land on. Moral of the day: Don't sleep with someone else's significant other?

I see my Grandpa holding me when I was just a little tyke, spinning me around in his arms. Then my mom was in the hospital embracing my new baby brother in her arms with a sweet, Loving smile on her face. A flash of the huge train set I discovered under the tree from Santa my first Christmas in Germany. The time my dad gave me a hug for hitting a homerun in little league. My very first kiss in a movie theater in Kansas, to a girl named Melanie. And it seems to go on and on while time is virtually standing still.

When your Life passes before your eyes, do you only see the good times? Are we that selective, or are they just your strongest memories put on display with God editing out the bad for you so it can be judged by itself?

I see a light at the end of it all, but I don't feel the presence of the divine. For some reason I feel fear. A fear that encompasses my whole being letting me know, without saying, that I am in for some serious soulful purging.

I hear the ocean before I feel the water crashing into my body. Am I dead? Oh no! Hell no! I feel something wrong. Damn! It makes me take quick shallow breaths while it pulsates, shooting pains through my body. It is a better feeling than the darkness I just came from, but reality is way too much for me to handle right now. I try to raise my head but cannot move. The water feels icy on my numb skin.

* * *

The next thing I know, I am in an ambulance. I hear the sirens first. It is always the sound that wakes us, I think. I look at the guy's face above me. I see his mouth fabricate a few words, "What's your name?" I pass out again.

* * *

Where am I? I am in a crematorium case, or on a morgue rack. I must be dead. I guess I am not going to Heaven yet. No floating above my body sensation either. This sucks so far! I hear someone yell, "Don't move." A door at my feet opens and someone slides me out. So, this is what a CT scan is like. I guess I am not dead yet, but I feel myself slipping away.

I wake again to the sounds of voices circling around me. I see people in fuzzy pastel hues of green, pink, and white. They come and go. Every now and then I make out something someone is saying, "He has suffered mild parietal shear injuries to the right cranial lobe." I think to myself, What? Fuck this, I have to work tomorrow, you quacks!

WTF . . . ?

What-the-f.com should have been my screen name back then. I was lucky to even be able to say, "This hospital food sucks," let alone, "Give me some more Jell- O, please." We all have these minor inconveniences in Life, right? I hope yours is less painful than mine, and more rewarding as well.

Don't worry, there could be less *dramatis personae* involved, and it could be less of a traumatic event to make you strong. "What doesn't kill you makes you stronger." Is that saying really truthful? Or is that some psychobabble, because right now these circumstances I'm in might turn out to be an enduring challenge?

Paradoxically, I am finding that the powers that seem to make sure your challenges lie in direct inverse proportion to your true weakness, "The chain is only as strong as its weakest link" philosophy, is becoming true.

These are just lessons in Love for our hearts to learn and the parts to be played. Doomed to repeat until conquered. I keep hearing whispers around me, and I can't make out yet if they are real or in my head. Am I crazy or asleep?

* * *

I am starting to feel awake finally. A body is standing by my bed. Is it an apparition of some sort, an Angel? No, it is . . . Cindy? Wow, what a thing to wake up to in a hospital bed. She puts her hand on my forehead.

"Hey, baby, how are you? I got back from Greece yesterday and you weren't there, so I checked my messages at home and your brother said what happened. He is downstairs getting some coffee."

I try to sit up and feel instant pain, "OHHH! Damn."

"Don't move, silly, you're hurt."

I feel a little disoriented, "What is . . . wrong . . . with me?"

"I'm not sure, ask your brother when he gets back. You look fine to me, but I guess you have a brain injury and a few broken bones."

"How was . . . your trip?"

"Oh, D! We had so much fun, and I met the cutest Greek guy!"

"OKAY . . . okay, tell me . . . the details . . . later."

"I will have to, D, and I will show you pictures too!"

"Swell . . . let's . . . go . . . home?"

"No! I just came to see if you're okay, you're not well enough to leave yet."

"I have to . . . work . . . tomorrow."

"Your brother already called everyone for you baby. Everything is fine, just rest."

"What . . . ever."

My brother walks in and I turn my head to look at the body entering the room.

"Ooohhhh fuck!"

"Relax, soldier, you have a few herniated disks in your neck, so I wouldn't advise any sudden moves."

"Now . . . you tell me. When did you . . . get here?"

"As soon as I could. I flew in this morning. You've been out for a day and a half. They thought you might slip into a coma, but I guess not, huh?" He reaches out to pat me on the chest.

"You have to help me . . . get out of here."

"Oh no, you just keep your happy ass right there in that bed until they release you, or I'll bruise the other side of your brain myself."

"What?"

"You have a TBI."

"Speak . . . English."

"A traumatic brain injury."

"Riiigghhht, I'm fine."

"No, seriously, Bro, you're a little slow right now, you just don't know it, so relax and chill until the doctors come back to talk to us. Then we will know what is up."

"Head hurts! I have . . . a headache. Can I get aspirin . . . or . . . something?"

"I don't think that's going to do any good. They already have you on something."

"Well, I need, more of it." My head feels like it is in a vice and my neck is shooting pains like stinging needles up and down it. "You called . . . my clients?"

"Yeah, a few might come visit."

"Great . . ."

"But I wouldn't hold your breath."

"Fff . . . fuck . . . you. Ouch!"

"See what you get when you talk nasty?"

I start to laugh a little and I hurt even more. "OOooowwww!"

"Remember, you also have broken ribs so I wouldn't breathe too deeply either."

"Anything, else I don't know —"

Cin interrupts, "I can't take this, D! It's too much for me, I will be at home if you need me, sweetie. Just get better and have them call me if you need anything. I will come and take you home if you need me to. Miss you, baby,"

She kisses me on the lips. I can smell her perfume and taste her atrocious lip gloss. Then she kisses me on my forehead and her boobs are so big that they brush across my face when she does like I am getting a lap dance right there in my hospital bed. It would be a cheap thrill, if I weren't in so much pain and maxed out on her already. She sashays to the door in her pink "f-me" pumps, blows me a kiss, and waves goodbye with her little girl smile.

My brother grins and says, "Yeah, there is something else you should know. Cindy is a complete blonde."

"No shit, Sherlock, try again."

"Okay, why are the cops waiting to talk to you when you wake up?"

"For real?"

"No, for fake."

"Umm, are they outside?"

"No, they are still in the cafeteria. They'll be up soon."

"Fuck, I don't know." Then it slowly dawns on me. I am having serious trouble remembering any of the details of the days before. It is a complete blank, or a haze of choppy, foggy moments.

"Sammy?" I mutter.

"Yep, that's it. I heard the fat one mention his name."

"Shit."

He gets up and looks out the door, "What?"

"Go with Cindy . . . in my mattress . . . an envelope. Uhhh, take it—" I pass out again.

* * *

I wake up and there are two guys in cheap suits hovering over me like vultures.

"Sir, sir, can you hear me?"

"Huh?"

"We need to ask you a few questions." The fat guy pushes his badge in my face like I am blind.

"Uh-huh . . ."

"Do you know if Mr. Luigi had any enemies, or did he mention if anyone had threatened him or his family to you."

"What?" I am completely annoyed.

The younger, skinny one steps forward. They remind me of Abbott and Costello. "Sir, do you know about Sammy being involved in any illegal activities?"

Even in my state I almost tell him off. "Nooo!"

The fat one gives him a dirty look and puts his hand in the air to stop him. "Well, Devon, we will be in touch. If you remember anything give us a call. I'll leave my number right here next to you."

Good cop, bad cop routine or just stupid, I can't tell. "Thanks."

They leave and in come the doctors. It is a group of three in pastel green. The older guy is the only one who speaks, "How are you feeling?"

"Like shit."

"That's understandable."

"Can I go?"

"A speech therapist will give you some tests and if you pass them, you can check out tomorrow evening. You will be in pain for a while and not able to do much, mobility wise. I have referred you to a local brain trauma clinic in Northridge and you will have to wear a neck brace for at least a month minimum."

"Oh, is that all?"

He chuckles, "Your brain has been shaken up and

needs rest, so I firmly suggest you lay low for at least a week and then you should start the clinic to rehabilitate any weaknesses the injury may have caused the right pre-frontal cortex and right rear lobe of your brain."

"Sure doc, whatever you say."

"We will check on you in the morning." He leaves with his entourage of intern cronies and I fade out to my previous dreamlike state.

THE UNRAVELING
AND THE BRAIN CLINIC

MAY 25

I am starting to recall strange days gone by. Is it from getting my grey matter jolted or is it the drugs they got me on? Actually, Vicodin doesn't induce weird memories. I think it was the near-death thing. I saw my Life pass by and thought that was it. I guess I'm not done here and have some more things to do? I keep seeing a future of a wife and a kid somewhere else, another place, or city. I cannot see their faces, but I know what they are supposed to represent. I am happy and successful.

Is this really a premonition or a cruel trick? God must have a sense of humor to tease me about this in the state I'm in. If this didn't happen every time I nodded off, I would just want to cash it in. Play some Russian roulette and say sayonara. What will I do now? Sammy is dead. I just lost Kris and Shawn. Amanda is leaving next week to shoot a movie in Prague. Ryan is never here, and Jason is going to the Pacific soon. I just lost my base training gym of five years after that fight with my prick of a manager who won't take me back now, especially since I am inoperable to train any clients at least for a month or two, at best! What will become of me?

* * *

I wake up again, only to realize that this place reminds me of when I got my tonsils removed as a kid in Kaiserslautern, Germany. It is the only other time I have ever been hospitalized. That was when my dad was in the Army. We were stationed at Hahn Air Force Base. He had a secret clearance and was working with Vulcan Missile Systems.

Those were the good old days, I think. We didn't get into fights back then. I was a good boy and not the rebel I later became after moving all the time. We moved about every two years, and after a while, I just started doing more daring, crazier stuff so I would be accepted by the "in crowd" of boys at each new place we moved to.

I eventually always joined sports because the jocks always seemed to have it good no matter where I went. They got the girls. The teachers were nicer to them. The local community treated them well. Especially in the smaller towns we lived in. I guess I became who I am out of survival, nature versus nurture.

I was much more of a shy, introverted, artistic boy growing up, but it got killed off from lack of support. Society only supports art on a top tier level, and mostly in metropolitan areas. When you live in towns under a hundred thousand in the Midwest you have to play football, wrestle, baseball, and whatnot, to be cool. You just didn't have other options. These days, kids are more independent. Back then you couldn't join a band, become a photographer, or become a poet unless it was for school, and then you became an instant nerd, or a bullied reject. In tiny rural places, this is not condoned by the rough and tumble men who run the good-old-boy network, and their kids, that they influence by affluence.

Even in towns like this, money and ignorance are the prominent catalysts for control. Control by fear. I lived my teen years in fear. Fear of not being accepted by the new kids, parents, teachers, coaches, Father, and myself.

We are always hardest on ourselves when we do not feel we are Loved. Who else can you blame as a kid if you don't? It is why teenage suicide is no joke. It was a dark time growing up and I am glad it's over, but now I am right back there because I can feel in my gut that it is time to go. I have to leave. There is nothing more for me here. I hate the thought of starting over again just like I did so many times before. Life goes on. I guess this is the lesson I have to learn.

I am moving rather slow as Cin walks alongside me to the car. I have been released and am free to go now since they have wheeled me out in a damn wheelchair to the front double doors first. No one came to see me, thank God! That would have been embarrassing. Although does anyone really even care? Not in LA. Not unless you're family. Otherwise, most people either have bystander apathy, are too self-involved, and/or squeezing as much as possible into their multitasked Life already.

Anyway, I have been told to see a neurologist, a neuropsychology specialist, a spine specialist, ophthalmologist, and an occupational therapist for starters. Not to mention, I am supposed to go to that damn brain trauma clinic for an unspecified amount of time. It still hurts to breathe. I feel like an old man who used to be a prizefighter hobbling around.

My thoughts seem to take longer to organize. Simple things like deciding what to wear and what to do next, are obscure and fuzzy. I drift off a lot in my head for no reason at all. I'm fine though, fine, just fine.

"Are you all right? Do you want to grab a bite to eat?" Cindy asks me like I am a five-year-old.

"No, just take me home." Appetite is nonexistent when you are on painkillers and being around people makes me feel very anxious now. I hate wearing this stupid neck brace and the attention it draws. I am not used to this. I am used to being strong, solid, and driven. I feel wimpy and soft. This sucks!

* * *

While I have faded in and out the past few days, I have not been a contributor of clarity to anything other than my own reinforcement of checking out of that place as soon as freakin' possible. And to think I was once premed bound? I even took all those clinical nutrition, biology, and organic chemistry classes. It was during a college work-study program in Administration for the Portland Veteran's Hospital that I came to the conclusion that I can't stand hospitals and that if I was ever to be an enforcer of health, that I would have to do it in a different field.

I'm leaving this place, and with it only the smallest amount of lucidity that I am living in a more primal state of survival right now. "Whatever it takes," is my motto, and it is taking all my brainpower to focus on the most idiosyncratic things.

The only thing I feel in this state right now is that sense of fear, which comes knocking at your door when the wind is knocked out of your sails for a spell. This is a new fear of the unknown. I do consciously know that I have no other choice but to be "agile, versatile, overcome, adapt, and survive," like my first permanent duty staff sergeant use to sternly say. If it had to be done, then it was. There was no room for "no" to enter the mental process, and I must do this!

Denial is a funny thing though. It tricks you into seeing a mirage of nothingness. There is no mirror reflection. You see no addiction, problem, or weakness before you. You only see the fact that you are lying to yourself after that quintessential defining moment kicks in. This moment can be as subtle as a bag of bricks to the face, or as peaceful as a dozen Angels humming a lullaby.

Unfortunately, as much as I am trying to do the latter, I am sent the slam dunk method from the Universe. This will be the time you look back and are glad you got hit in the guts and had to take the pain, right? Yeah, yeah, yeah . . . I am either going to be my own salvation or my own demise of self-propagated victimhood.

I have always done my best in this Life, and hoped for the sun, moon, stars and planets to align properly enough for me to move forward with whatever good fortune I might have during any given amount of beneficial circum-stances. This has been my unwritten and unspoken philos-ophy thus far.

Right now, uncertainty has bestowed a new gift upon me. The realization that nobody here cares! Why should I stay? I will take this wounded persona and rebuild the ark somewhere else. I can do it. Everyone here is looking for the next stepping-stone or b.b.d. There is no loyalty. No roots in LA, I have no reason to stay. They will forget about me in a week.

I care about others, but my phone is not ringing off the hook. Well, there has been a lot of empathy expressed from my clients to my brother when he called them. I have heard some nice messages inquiring about my health and wellbeing, but I need to repair and get strong and move forward.

I think I know what to do, but I am having trouble doing simple math equations and I have patches of memories from recently acquired files that must have been swept away from the hard drive. It is a little scary because I don't believe it is there, but it is. I am firing those axons and neurons, but the connections are not meeting as optimally as before or picking the same patterns of circuitry.

No one here in LA to help me, other than a slightly reliable Cin. No family here to ask simple questions for unbiased answers, to help me decide basic things. I don't need them anyway. I will be fine tomorrow. I am just tired because I need rest. I will start work in a few weeks. Wow, that might be weird in a neck brace if my anxiety doesn't subside. I can do it though.

But why am I staying here? Maybe I . . . I need to go see my brother and have a night of sake and sushi and mentally pummel this crap to oblivion. We will process this stuff 'til the cows come home and figure it out. The doctor said that I cannot fly yet, though.

* * *

It is technically against the law to operate a motor vehicle after an incident has rendered you unconscious for any length of time, but obviously I don't have a personal chauffeur. I felt like passing out while driving here, but I was so full of anxiety from concentrating on the traffic that it kept me going. Consequently, I arrived at my brain trauma clinic mentally exhausted.

Upon arriving I found out, to my blessing and horror at the same time, that although I am slower from healing my brain right now, I am much better off than some of the others going through this process as well. Some of these people are seriously more damaged than I am, and this is not helping me to stay.

I am lucky as hell. These patients cannot even do simple things that a week or month ago would have been routine humdrum daily tasks. I am thinking compassion is my newest friend right now, even though my injured self really wants to try to sprint back out the door. No, you can deal. Just deal. It will be over soon. Go through the motions and just get through it fast. Kick ass!

We're going to do what the nurse practitioner/therapist says, "Play games!" Great, just great! Harold is going to be heartbroken when I tell him I am busting out after lunch since I have been showing him how to remake coffee in the kitchen of the clinic we are in. He must miss it like me too. Our heads just haven't been able to handle the full effects of that caffeine rush like before. Now, a half a cup starts my nervous system to tense up and pulls my cramped muscles in new directions everywhere by my spinal cord. This causes everything to knot up even more, and ache from the increased inflammation.

Harold was taking a sunny Sunday cruise on a brand-new Harley he had been waiting to get his whole Life, and some negligent texting-while-driving idiot rear ended him into this clinic. He is impaired physically, as well as mentally. Where he once walked upright and in proper alignment, he now bends and moves like Cro-Magnon Man. I like him. You can tell he was pretty laid back and cool.

There is also a really nice girl here named Rebecca who saw me park as she was being helped out of a van in a wheelchair, and now says she "wants to drive my car." Rebecca wants to drive any car so bad. Poor thing got an aneurysm in her brain, for no apparent reason, on the day of her sweet sixteenth birthday and was supposed to go get her license the next day. Now, she will have to wait a long time. Half of her head is shaved. You can tell she is a little insecure about the stitches where they cut into the side of her skull. Can't blame her. It reminds me of Frankenstein or something.

The therapists are all nice, middle-aged, married women of moderate plumpness. They run the games, questionnaires, physical therapy, etc. I find it hard to endure it all. I am not able to take it seriously. I don't need to be here. I want to go home and just sleep it away. Not looking forward to the stressful drive home though . . .

* * *

I had a dream about Wendy last night, extremely vivid. I was standing at the edge of a cliff and there was a giant Sequoia forest below, and every tree was cut off evenly at the top like an enormous blade had leveled them with one smooth stroke. I couldn't see the floor under the trees. It was a pitch-black abyss that went on forever. I needed to get to the other side but the only way across the vast canyon was to hop from tree to tree. I started out very confident but with each succeeding jump, the trees got farther apart until I got out in the middle and looked down and froze. I looked back and there were no trees to go back on, only forward. Then it ended abruptly when the Pterodactyls I was shooting with a bow and arrows the night before, started to swoop down from above. In that dream, which comes and goes, I have one less arrow every time!

What does this have to do with Wendy? I don't really know; it is just a hunch. She keeps popping up as the reason even though it defies linear logic. If I would have died, would I have said all those things you need, or want, to say to the ones you Love? Maybe this is a sign. I should take my meager savings, and just bust out of town. The dream could be a message to go see her in Colorado. Maybe this was meant to humble me enough to go and beg her to come back, that I can't live another day without her, that I saw this while recovering and I want to work it out? That I still Love her? And I could stop on the way to see my bro in Aspen.

Scott is tapping me on the shoulder. Scott is a new applicant to the clinic today. Of course, he will be accepted because they don't turn you away, but he is a peculiar one. He looks like he should be teaching Physics and talks like a professor but cannot execute the simplest of things. I think he has spatial challenges. He tries to walk through a space too small to fit, and he has trouble with things like Legos or blocks, or games that have to be intertwined together to make something. He got tapped on the forehead too hard by a miss-swung golf club from his son. Who would have thought that would put him in this place? I hope he changes back, or his son will grow up with a guilt complex and in foster care because I overheard a counselor in the next room mention that he is the only living parent.

I told them this is my last week. I'm outta here. I can't take the idea of getting better in an environment that reinforces my belief that I am unable to perform daily duties. I'll go home and play some video games, computer chess, read, write, and whatever else I have to do to fake it until I make it back to normal cerebrally. No one can tell anyway unless they ask me too many complex questions in a row. That, and math problems are what causes me mental malfunctions. Since all my injuries are internal and I have been taking about ten plus herbs and supplements daily, haven't been eating a lot and mostly a vegetarian diet, had a drink or coffee, I look really healthy. My skin is even kind of glowing.

Tomorrow is the big day to get released from this place anyway. If, and when, I pass my final examination with the head Dr. Neurology lady I will get back to working on a normal routine like before all this non-holistic, post-injury, half-ass medical crap. Other than being diagnosed with cognitive impairments, slow visual tracking and response time, and other mental and physical dysfunction's blah, blah, blah—I am fine. Seriously, fine . . .

THE FUNERAL—
GET ME OUTTA' HERE!

MAY 31

People are coming up to me and asking me, over and over, why I am wearing a neck brace, and "if I am alright?" They should be talking about Sammy.

It is a large assemblage of people, among some of them are celebrities who speak. Larry King even gets up to say a thing or two during the eulogy. There was a full page in Variety and the *Hollywood Reporter* with his picture expressing their condolences this week as well.

I am still on Vicodin. It makes me more relaxed, talkative, and less achy when I have to move. Otherwise, I would be neurotic and antisocial. Haven't been very sharp lately for some reason. It took me a while to just pick which suit to wear, and I only have three. I couldn't remember how to tie a tie either.

I just saw Sammy's lawyers before this. Believe it or not, he left me a few things from the weight room, and a rather decent amount of cash from a safety deposit box. Who would have thought? I had to sign an affidavit that I would keep my mouth shut, and that under no certain circumstances would anyone be told about this gift he had so generously left me from his living will.

I am amazed at the turnout. He knew a lot of very influential people from both coasts and foreign countries. You can tell by the accents and dress. I drift in and out of reality. It all seems like a dream, and I still have trouble wrapping my head around it.

The funeral is closed casket, thank God. I think I would squeeze out a tear or two if it weren't. Most of the women cry and some of the men do, too. It is a mass of sadness, and the vibe is queasy even though the coffins are all the same size, but there are too many, and it makes you feel sick to your stomach.

After it is over, I humbly say hello to his closest of kin and Mother. I mingle with a few others I have met at the house dinners and start to make my way to the car, dizzy and exhausted by it all. I am almost there, and I see a man standing in front of it. He is the fat "good cop" from the hospital.

"Hello, how are you?" he says as I unlock the door.

"Tired and depressed."

"That's too bad because I wanted to know if you could come down to the station and—"

"No."

"I understand your upset. Maybe we could swing by in a few hours and pick you up and—"

"Did I stutter? No!"

"Well, I tried being nice. You are going to be subpoenaed when this all goes down. Don't you want to be on the right side when it does?"

"Fuck off, and have a good day, sir."

"You're going to burn when they charge you for hiding evidence, you little shit!"

I get in and leave. His family hasn't even been covered with dirt yet, and they are accusing him of foul play. He's the one who is dead! They should be going after the killers, not bothering me. What do I know that could possibly help them?

* * *

I come home early to rest now, or otherwise I completely wear out and am a worthless mass of mental mush. As I pull into my subterranean parking area, I notice a car pull up out front and park with two guys in it. I didn't even see them following me. I am not my usual self. I am lacking awareness. The gate opens, and I drive in and go upstairs.

The phone rings, and it is the front door to my condominium building. I make Cin answer it.

"Hello, this is Cindy." She looks at me and mouths, "Are you here?" I shake my head "no," forgetting about my neck. "Oww."

"No, he's not in right now. May I take a message? No, that was my boyfriend, he just stubbed his toe on the bed, sorry, okay I will, bye."

She turns to me and says, "They said they need to take you down to the station and ask you a few questions, look at some photos, and it would be in your best interest to cooperate."

"What? You're kidding me, right?"

"No, that's what they said, sweetie. How are you feeling?"

"Like shit as usual, tired. If they ever come by when I am not here, do not let them in."

"They already did."

"What?!"

"I was going to tell you when you got home right now, D!"

"Why did you let them in?"

"They had a search warrant; wow, I feel like I am on that show you watch sometime on TV."

"You saw it?"

"Yeah, it was for real, baby, but why would they do that?"

"I don't know yet."

"Well, you better find oooouut."

"No shit, did they take anything with them?"

"No, but they knew what they wanted."

"What?"

"They kept asking about any documents from Mr. Luigi?"

"Oh shit!" I bolt to the hiding place in my room. The room is tossed and torn apart, but the air conditioning vent is still intact, and the screws I painted over to make it look like it has never been opened are still fresh and unscarred, so I know they didn't open it. I run back out to Cindy.

"OOowww!"

"Slow down, cowboy, or are you forgetting you just had an accident?"

"No lecture. I need to go to the airport ASAP. I will pack, and you have to take me, I have to get out of here for a while, trust me!"

The roles are reversed, and Cindy is taking me to the airport. "I don't like this idea, D, what are you running from?"

"I am just getting away to clear my head, clear up some stuff, that's all."

"I don't know. You don't do things like this for no reason. I think you're up to something. When will you be back?"

"I don't know. Maybe never."

"What? You can't do that to me. I need you. What will

I do with your stuff? Who will walk my little baby when I am busy, or have coffee with me, or—"

"Easy, easy, I might be in danger. Do you want me to get killed?"

"No!"

"Then let me do this, and we'll see what happens, end of discussion!"

"Well, I'll miss you D."

"I'll miss you too, now concentrate on driving; you're making me nervous."

"Sorry."

"It's because of the accident. I can't help it."

"You're not supposed to fly, are you?"

"Not really?"

"Deeee!"

"I'll be fine, didn't I already say that? Now let me rest my brain, we'll talk at the airport, and make sure no one is following you."

"Yes, Dad. "

* * *

I sleep on the flight all the way there and get off the plane, only to wait two hours for my brother because he is on call. He is a kick-ass fireman in Aspen. He was probably saving someone's Life.

I once got mad at him for not being available for a phone interview for a "Brothers" episode on *Fear Factor*. I stood there in front of the casting directors like a dumbass for a half hour and walked out. When he finally called me, he apologized for not being available that hour, but he had just saved a little boy and his mother trapped in an overturned vehicle from dying. I had to eat it right then and there, and admit there are much bigger things in Life to sulk over.

He gets here, and looks a little worn.

"Hey, thanks for picking me up on such short notice."

"No worries. Why are you here?"

"What kind of welcome is that? Thought maybe you could use a sushi and sake partner about now. What do you say?"

"I'm beat."

"C'mon . . ."

"Alright, you're buying."

"That's the spirit!"

He toasts his full sake glass to mine, and powers down his first full cup. "Now, why are you here?"

"Those cops are looking for that envelope I had you hide for me, and I didn't know what to do? I even ran into them at Sammy's funeral. I am sick of LA, anyway. You know all those times I said I might move here and start over? Well, this may be it."

"Seriously?"

"Damn straight!"

"Well welcome aboard. Welcome to Tinseltown in the mountains. I don't know if it will be much different here for you, other than actual seasons, but I got your back until you get on your feet." We toast again and the food comes. "What will you do?"

"Don't know."

"I can talk with my Chief. Might be able to get you hired to teach CPR and first aid classes?"

"Sure."

"How are your skills? "

"Need to brush up a bit."

"Do it."

"Yes, sir!"

"Or you'll have to take some shit, local job on the slopes or something."

Aspen and
the Wendy Reunion

August 27

How right he was. I am working at the base of the gondola for the mountain during summer operation, and in training for the ski season to start later. The air is so clean and brisk, but I am quickly beginning to miss the perceived freedom I had when working in my previous job. I really was a slave to my client's schedules, but I told them what to do and had at least enough autonomy to believe I was in charge.

There is only one supervisor in charge of this cult-like group of employees, but they are micromanaged as if it is a communist country. They are in a constant state of paranoia too. They act like it is in the middle of the season already. They keep regurgitating war stories about how busy it will be, and how the owners will be here so everything has to be perfect. I want to throw up.

They remind me of those Hollywood assistants I used to sneer at, whenever I witnessed this, but they had no power over me, and now these people will run to their nearest supervisor like a baby with his/her thumb in their mouth if I even look at them cross-eyed. I don't know if I am cut out for the mile-high altitude Life. I mean, it definitely is "purple mountains and majestic skies," and when the leaves turn gold in the fall, it is gorgeous, but I don't really like skiing all that much.

I dig the snowmobiles though. Love to catch air on those babies early in the morning before anyone shows up. I take them to over eighty miles per hour, and I am on PCH again, albeit a snow-covered version, weaving in and out of trees instead of cars. You would think I would have learned my lesson, but I don't believe lightning will strike me twice in the same way, and I am not sleeping with anyone's wife right now. In fact, I am not sleeping with anyone. How sad. Sad enough to plan a trip to Boulder soon to see Wendy and reconnect with my soulmate, or so I thought.

* * *

I drive up to the house in the 'burbs of Boulder, and I am practically shaking like a leaf. She has agreed that we should talk. "Talk," whatever that means. I am bracing myself to see her new son that she conceived right after we split and popped out almost exactly nine months after. I know it is going to hurt, but I am obviously a sucker for punishment.

I park, and she comes right out with the little guy. He is a cutie, and I can't help but be nice to him.

"Hi, how are you?" she says as I try to give her a hug. She doesn't really respond, and I'm taken aback by this.

"I'm fine, are you okay with this?"

"Sure, yeah, I just haven't seen you in so long and it's a little weird so . . . Just give me a second."

I bend down to make friends, "Hey, little man—"

"You look really good. I forgot how handsome you are."
A compliment. I'm in. "Thanks, you look good too." A
quick response back to placate her in case she is just messing with me, as I discover I am still impaired when I look
into her absolutely enchanting, green eyes.

"Let's go in the living room and talk. My mom is going
to take Ben to the mall with her."

"Sure."

* * *

We are seated across from each other, and she is looking at me so sheepishly that I start to feel like I just beat
her although I have never hit a woman my entire Life. I
don't know my own strength, and pushed her down once
by accident, but otherwise believe domestic violence towards women are acts of complete cowardice.

I think she is still scared of me though because the last
time she was dropped off by "the other guy" in front of
our place, one late night after work, I was temporarily
insane. I was close to exploding. I wanted to let him know
I meant business and make him think twice, but it
backfired, puncturing my heart with the shrapnel.

She was gone the next day. Pregnant weeks later to a
schmuck who just wanted to get laid and take advantage
of her when she was drunk. He played it right and got the
goods. I swear there were bets riding on this one. Who
would get her?

I touch her hand, and she pulls it away. "Maybe this
was a bad idea," I softly suggest.

"No, I just don't know how to feel. I miss you, but I still
have a lot of things to figure out and—"

"Do you still Love me?" There I said it. No reason to
beat around the bush.

"I . . . Yes, I will always Love you but—"

"You're not in Love with me. Well, how 'bout those Bronco's? They look good this season, don't they?" I stand up. "You know, I really can't stay long, but it was great to see you and—"

She starts crying, "I'm soooo sorry. I didn't mean to hurt you so bad!" She goes from zero to one hundred and is in full sobbing mode now.

"Hey, hey stop. You don't have to do that. It is what it is." She doesn't respond. I want to hold her as it kills me to see her cry, even though it feels so good to hear her apologize with even a hint of remorse. I think I can die now. Mission accomplished.

She slowly raises her tear- soaked face and grabs my hand and holds it. The feeling of her hands on mine is almost enough to make me completely mentally distracted. I think about football to put me back in the right frame of mind.

"I am seeing a counselor, and I am making progress. I know it takes two, but I am taking responsibility for me, and I want to try again. Can you give me that?"

I am blindsided and surely didn't see that one coming. She might as well have stood up from her chair and given me a fierce uppercut.

She finally raises her eyes to mine, pulls me into her body, and gives me a soft, warm, slow hug. I am a lost puppy dog who has found his way home. I put my palms on both her cheeks, ever so delicately, and start to give her a small kiss on the lips, but she turns her head so that it falls on her cheek.

I immediately lose my spark. It makes me feel like I am kissing my mom goodbye. My instincts tell me that she is setting me up. Maybe I am overreacting and should have more compassion, but I don't trust her enough to go with it.

"What about Ben?"

"He's a great kid, and he seems to like you. I told him all about you, he's just really, really shy." That was the question she wanted to avoid. I can hear it in her tone.

"I'm sure he is, and he is a beautiful kid, got his mom's good looks, just wanted to know how he felt."

"He's a kid, he will adapt. He doesn't ever see his father anyway."

I can't take it anymore. I have bit my tongue long enough. "Another fatherless kid. Seems to be a pattern in your family."

She starts to cry again, "I am doing the best I can."

"I know, but he is not mine, and I don't think it is the same. I thought I could Love you both and it would be like before, but now I am realizing it's a little weird." I feel foolish and relieved at the same time.

"But . . . but you said . . . you said we could work it out!"

"Yes, I did, but I don't want to be the fool for Love, the schmuck who lost it, and the throwback, fall guy for you now, all in one lifetime. I'm sorry, really, really sorry."

I pull away and give her a kiss on the forehead, "I wish you the best."

I do not look back, and silently vow to leave my pain on her doorstep as I walk out.

I can hear her screaming and throwing things as I get in the car and drive away. That's it, get it out girl, you'll feel better tomorrow. I hope I do, too, because right now, I feel as if something has been permanently lost. Like I am an amputee. I just let go of my supposed soul mate. My biggest and brightest hope for a normal future of familial happiness in the Midwest.

It felt as if I had been made the emasculated, male

mockery of misfortune before today's events came to pass. Now I feel exonerated and empty at the same damn time! What will I do now? Life has thrown me a curve ball again. I swung and missed while aiming at the lights for a home run with the bases loaded.

I drive back to Aspen like a zombie. My mind shutdown from what just went down and closed off to any more logical thoughts. I feel vacuumed inside. Like my heart has been lipoed of all the fatty history. Nothingness and . . . numb.

The Eye-Opener
and the Opportunity

I haven't worked out for a long time, and my brother keeps twisting my arm to go to the gym with him, but it reminds me of the former world I have escaped. I envision it will be like revisiting a bad dream. I keep telling him "I'll clean up and go tomorrow," like a heroin addict every time he brings it up.

He gets pissed and storms off without me. When I hear the door slam, I take my sorry ass to the fridge, grab a brew, and pop on the telly.

My motivation has become unmotivated. I lack the will to do anything but go to my shitty job and come home to my regular-scheduled programming. My highlight of the day is when I catch a rerun episode of *Law and Order: SVU*, or something which requires no thought at all like *Pawn Stars* or *Ridiculousness*. I sleep all the time and go to bed early, but I am always tired. I have hardly any appetite to speak of.

I cannot be late one more time in the next six months or

I'll get canned. My supervisor and I hate each other, and if it wasn't for my bro pulling a few strings, and putting his good name out there for me, I would kick his narrow ass from here to New York City and back.

I guess you could say I am missing something, but I really don't want anything and don't care. I have been humbled by the wrath of God and would appreciate if the entire planet would f-ing leave me alone to just be, thanks. I have given my best, and I might just utilize Dr. Kevorkian's philosophy and practices someday, so mind your own business, and piss off, as my old client Mr. Jones used to say.

* * *

Last night was an eye-opener of prolific proportions, though. My bro came home and tipped over my bed, drill sergeant style, like I was back in hellish basic training.

I got up, dazed and confused, and he yelled, "Get dressed. Get in the truck, now!"

I did it. I knew he was serious. He had never spoken to me like that before. I am his big brother. I got in the truck, and he never said a word the whole way there.

When we pulled up, it was chaos.

My brother looked at me with intensity like I have never seen before and said, "Put away your sorry, sad sack of shit, and do something for somebody else for a change!"

He got out and left me sitting there. I looked ahead and saw a building burning to the ground, and another one next to it on fire. The first building was an apartment for lower-income housing, and the two next to it were a day-care center and a children's nursery.

On the way there, I heard some talk on his handheld radio. The dispatcher was speculating that the fire may have been caused by some tree-hugging, preservationists that were trying to stop the nearby construction in order to save the forests and wildlife.

It must have spread too fast and became a hazard, claiming lives instead of the impressionable good it was supposed to impose on the overzealous, powermongers who own the surrounding mountain resorts, and intend to keep on expanding and making more money than God.

I didn't know what to do, but I found that they needed all the help they could get. Some of the kids were injured, either from smoke inhalation or burns after being trapped by the fire in the upper floors.

I followed my brother and started to give CPR or first aid to the smoke victims. My bro wasn't even on duty anymore. He had just finished a nonstop, forty-eight-hour shift, but once you're a public servant that just doesn't matter.

We saved as many as possible and worked all night 'til dawn. When the sun came up, we were standing on the burnt down nursery looking for any missing persons and helping frantic parents.

I was overwhelmed by it all. I just stood there in awe, and as I looked down at my feet, I found to my extreme horror that I was standing on the body of a little girl who was burnt to a crisp. She was so charred that she was unrecognizable and camouflaged by her charcoal coloring. From that moment I woke up. I had many other moments to do so, but in my exhausted and emotional state, this one hit me like a Mack truck going at full speed. I was forever changed.

* * *

The next day I woke up, thanked God for the new day, fixed my bro breakfast, left it on the counter, and went to the gym.

It was somewhat of a nostalgic experience. I had forgotten

the things that were embedded in my senses: the smell of the sweat, the smell of the leather on the equipment, the clanging of the chrome dumbbells, the iron weight stacks slamming together on the machines, the hum of the treadmills and cardio equipment, the adrenaline and endorphin releases.

I had lost that. I missed it. I was dying from exhaustion as I pushed through it, straining to sweat out all the bad toxins, and subconsciously believing to shed the skin of the apathetic Devon to embrace the new. I relearned what it felt like to be a neophyte again, and my compassion for them returned out of my inability to physically fly high like before. It was great!

Afterwards, I stopped by the old "quicker-picker-upper" place. Good ole Starbucks. I ordered two coffees for my brother and me.

I knew the surprise breakfast would not be complete without his favorite coffee hand delivered to his bedside. He is addicted to caramel lattes, and acts like they are becoming an extinct, limited resource.

I was waiting patiently for my order when she walked in. In all the coffee joints "in all the world she had to walk into mine." I know Kevin Costner, Jeff Bezos, Tom Cruise, and a bunch of other people have houses here, but damn.

I was in such a good mood flirting with the local girl at the cash register that I didn't even notice her. Calista stopped dead in her tracks, and so did everyone else in the store as she just locked onto me. I kept talking, and then laughed at my own joke, but the deafening silence forced my attention to focus on what it was that had caused such a non-commotion. You could hear a pin drop.

I looked over my shoulder, and there she was in her big, white sunglasses, Ugg boots, skintight jeans, and a white, cashmere turtleneck sweater. She looked unbelievably hot.

If I hadn't regained my mojo, I might have dropped the ball but being that I was slightly back on top, I cocked my head ever so slightly and said, "Hey, princess, where have you been all my Life?" Why I would pull something like that out of my ass at that moment, I do not know?

It worked though, I guess, because she walked right up to me, took off her sunglasses, shook her hair back like a slow-motion Beyonce video moment, put both her hands on my shoulders, like we were a couple, and retorted, "Looking for you . . ."

Then she kissed me on the cheek and hugged me. The whole place started clapping, and I was frozen. I must have stood there motionless for a few minutes while she ambled over to the counter and ordered a bunch of non-caffeinated cocktails.

She looked over her shoulder at me and winked while doing this, and mouthed, "I need to talk to you."

I casually waited while hooking up my Columbian Roast, venti drip with a little half-n-half and brown sugar, at the condiments table. I take a sip to see if it's suited to my palatable perfection.

She floats over and says, "I called you, but you didn't call back. I think that's very rude, and you deserve a spanking."

"Really, well I was temporarily unavailable."

"Well, I hope you are available now because I need you. I need you professionally, I mean."

"What?"

"I want to hire you. I am up for the part of a lifetime and in order to nail it, I have to be in the best shape of my Life. I won't be able to do it with anyone else. I need the best. I have seen you in action, in more ways than one, I might add, and I know you're the guy to keep me stimulated and not stray."

"Is that a question or an answer?" I ask.

"I need to get into kick-ass shape, and the fact that I ran into you here solidifies it. You are the one. When can we start?"

"I don't do that anymore."

"What? Wrong answer."

"I am sorry, I can't help you. Find someone else, I left that job in LA." I turn and grab my brother's finished caramel latte off the counter, say "Thank you," to the barista, and start to head out the door.

I am outside, and the whole place is still locked on us like an intense tennis match as she immediately comes outside and blocks me from opening the car door.

"What are you doing now that is so important that you can't help me out? Look, I am serious."

"You are spoiled. That's what you are, and I am done working with people like you." I reach by her for the door handle, and in the reflection of the glass, I notice a little girl standing next to her, and for a brief millisecond in time I flashback to the girl I so sadly discovered earlier, that very same morning, at the fire.

It was Calista's daughter, and she turns to her and puts her hand on her head. "Mommy will be with you in a second, honey."

Calista turns back to me. "She is upset because her new friend she just met died in that fire last night, and this is a new one for her. Look, I'm sorry, I'll leave you alone. I just thought—"

"When do you want to start?"

She is actually caught off guard for a second as she pauses to search for an answer. "Umm, tomorrow. I am all yours."

"Okay eight a.m. sharp, no excuses, no complaining, and do everything I tell you to, or the deal is off, and I'm ghost."

"Yes, sir, thank you."

I move towards the little girl and ask, "What's your name?" "Michelle," she says, and as she bravely reaches out, I shake her little hand.

"Nice to meet you, Michelle, I am Devon." Calista smiles at me. I get in the truck and shut the door. Calista picks up Michelle and knocks on the window. I lower it.

"Why don't you come over for dinner tonight."

"Thank you, I appreciate it, but if we're going to be seriously working together then I don't think it's a good idea." I give my little kiddie a wave, "Bye Michelle."

Michelle is so cute, she is irresistible. I guess my conscience is working overtime in thinking that if I help Calista, it will justify my guilt for that burnt to death, little girl I found myself standing on only hours ago, or maybe it was just Jerry Maguire syndrome. I'm not sure, but either way my heart went out to the because. It overtook me and commandeered my rebellious angst and obnoxious desire to blow off the whole situation.

As I drive away and get farther and farther from it, I start to rejoice in it all. I would have given my left pinky finger, Yakuza-style, to have this opportunity in Hollywood before I moved here and dumped that whole scene. Now it falls back in my lap.

Is it destiny or is a demonic haunt following me? Is it like that Lauren Hill lyric, "After winter must come spring," or is my beloved Calista the Antichrist? I don't have a clue. Maybe this is what my prophetic, Guru Chick meant by letting go would allow new things to come into my Life? I gave myself the ultimate blessing of closure with Wendy and now this? Regardless, I feel I am back! I will kick this LA Queen's ass and be done with it, if she can even hang.

* * *

I am at the gondola, and in a good mood for a change, as I finish handling the night-skiing, prep shift that has to be perfectly executed by the time the season starts so no one gets sued, m y boss shows up. I acknowledge his presence by saying, "Hello," and expect him to leave me alone to do my job, but he just stands there and stares at me.

I blow it off for a little while, choosing to ignore him, with his crazy eyes and strange demeanor. I continue to pleasantly go about my business. For once, my "customer service" and interaction with the guests, riding it for a bite in the restaurant and great view at the top, is altruistic and sincere.

After about five more minutes of ogling, I realize he is hawking me for either two reasons: A) He is checking me out like an hors d'oeuvre appetizer, and has had a secret closeted crush on me since day one or, B) He is about to go postal on me.

I have had about enough, so I casually look his way and ask, "Can I help you with something?"

He instantly lunges at me like a bobcat with rabies. I am caught off guard and fall into a moving car, hitting my head on the seat. It almost knocks me out. I see stars, but I manage to jump out right before it leaves the dock.

I am dizzy, and he is waiting. I can smell the liquor on his breath. His eyes are filled with disdain and hate. Must be a theme in my Life that when a male authority figure to me gets drunk, he just has to come find me and take out his shit on me, because it has happened before. I know we haven't exactly seen eye to eye, but I really doubt it warrants this kind of attack. Oh well, here we go.

I am not mad at all, so I begin to take a beating until he starts to wear himself out. The man is more out of shape than I am right now, and hits like a wuss. He is panting now, so I grab him by the throat to spook him a bit and let him know I am in control. He takes a couple more swings, but I stiff-arm him and there is hardly any real contact. He finally stops.

"What is your major malfunction, asshole?!" I yell. I was supposed to say, "soldier," at the end of that, but he is hardly worthy of being called something that respectful.

"You're fired."

I push him down onto the floor and give him a good hard look. I start to walk over to him, and he starts to inch backward like a crab. The shoe is on the other foot, and his true cowardice is rearing its ugly head.

"I said, you're fired!"

"I heard you the first time, you piece of shit!" I make a quick, fake lunging motion at him with my body, and he scurries backwards in fear.

I force myself to walk away, even though I want to take out all the frustration I had with the last boss I said that to, on this guy as well. I don't because I am scared to let go. I might really hurt him. My brother would be disappointed with my lack of maturity and control. This guy is not worth it. I guess in my mind, it seems like I always end up working for pieces of shit.

PART II
LOVE

Michelle and Bobby

September 4

I arrive the next morning early and ready. I shake off my nervousness and mentally prepare as I walk up to the door.

The house is set amongst all the other five-million-plus vacation homes in the giant, gated homestead. They all have architecturally distinct exteriors, and each one has a completely different floor plan, but they all look the same to me. In LA, these homes would be another couple mill on top of their asking price, just because of the size of the real estate.

This community is very special though because it is all-inclusive. It has: a guard, private mailing center, on-call fireman and paramedics, a road crew, a shuttle service, spa, and lastly, a huge recreation center, fully equipped for the kids to do anything they want.

They especially wanted to add their own Starbucks, but were denied the rights, even though they were more than willing to fork over the cash of some astronomical amount. You see, the chain conglomerate is a corporation. You can't buy it as a franchise. So, they built their own private coffee shop too, but it is still not as good as Starbucks is. Hence, the reason the higher-ups still bust into town to get their favorite cup of coffee, and why I even ran into Calista in the first place.

These people are even more eccentric than LA people. The board of directors up here decided to repave the asphalt at ten thousand dollars a foot (it's heated for the winter ice and snow!) because one guy got a chip in his Aston Martin Vanquish windshield on the former road one day and made a stink. Meanwhile many people in America can't afford health care, or higher education for their children.

I knock. No one answers for a minute then the door opens with a "house on haunted hill" creepy, slowness. I have to look down at once like a tiny mouse has just pushed it open. To my surprise, Michelle is standing there.

"Hello," she says as she looks up at me.

"Hey, little one, how are you?"

"Fine, Mommy is in the other room, I will take you to her."

"Thank you."

I walk through the house with Michelle as my escort, holding my hand and guiding me through a maze of rooms, when a boy jumps out from behind a sofa and shoots me with a super soaker. I am stunned.

Michelle screams, "Bobby, stop!"

Bobby runs away, laughing like a hyena. I am soaked and perplexed, but what are you gonna do?

We get to the room, and Calista is on the phone arguing with someone. I look down at Michelle who is still holding my hand. "Mommy will be with you in a moment. She is taking care of some business at home in LA."

"Thank you." It is all I can keep saying to this preadolescent secretary-in-training, who acts like an adult.

"If you need anything—a Coke, water, or whatever— let me know, byyyye."

"Bye-bye."

She shuts the door as she leaves. Calista turns to me and gives me the one finger up for the one-minute sign. I nod in agreement, but I am already dismayed at her lack of preparation.

She is standing there in a paper-thin, white, silken nightgown and robe. If it wasn't for the early morning sun shining through her outfit from the giant windows and revealing those sleek, voluptuous curves on her svelte body, I would be growing more impatient every second I have to wait. I watch her move back and forth like a cat while she intensely corresponds with her agent.

"What do you mean he won't do scale for a role like that? Tell him that if he doesn't commit today, I am giving the part to that new kid at CAA, what's his name? Yeah, him. I don't give a shit what they think, the producers are in agreement with me. I can run with it this time, I'm the one who got the green light on this bitch, it's my fucking option, and that's how it's going to be . . . Thank you, Okay . . . Five o'clock, Okay . . . Bye."

She turns to me like a seductress in heat, but her expression instantly changes. "Why are you all wet?"

"A mischievous little boy named Bobby?"

"Oh, I am sorry about that, he doesn't have any other boys to play around with on this street, so he gets totally out of hand when he sees a male—"

"It's fine really, so about you, your goals."

"You know, I don't think I can do this today, I have to—"

"You know what? That's okay, I don't think this is going to work out anyway, no pun intended." I grab my bag, sling it over my shoulder, and reach for the doorknob.

"Whoa, wait a second. What's up? I'll pay you for this session. I just have to take care of some last-minute business."

She walks towards me. Her top blows back a bit as she does, and I can see her breasts. I am momentarily transfixed as she closes it and stops inches in front of me. I can smell her. She is not even wearing a touch of makeup, and I still think she is the most beautiful woman I have ever laid eyes on.

"Now look, Handsome. I am sorry, but this is the movie I want you to train me for. Just give me one more day. I will make it up to you, okay? Just tell me what you want?"

What a loaded question. *I could lose myself in your bosom,* is what I'm thinking. "I want you to work out!"

"I will sweetie, how 'bout tonight, we can work out and then go for a bite at Larkspur. I hear they have a to die for filet, with seasonal-grilled Matsutake mushrooms."

What do I do? Talk about cognitive dissonance. I am torn between putting my foot down and actually sharing an intimate evening with her. The client is always right, is the customer service motto, and she hasn't really broken any rules yet, but I need to set a precedent for her as well.

"When?"

"I have the phone conference at five so, six? Let's work out at six, and I will take you to dinner, my treat, at eight, eight thirty. Deal?"

"Sure, then we can talk about your goals and every-thing else."

"Great—done, see you then."

I feel lucky as hell, and cheap at the same time, but I keep myself composed and walk out not giving her a chance to figure me out. I lead myself out. The kids are nowhere to be found.

I open the front door and catch a glimpse of Bobby hiding by the car. I leave the door swung open, then walk back to the kitchen, and rifle through the cupboards until I find a plastic pitcher and fill it with water.

I go back and run out the door at full speed to where he is hiding beside the vehicle. He starts to yell as I dowse him with every drop and runs inside like a startled spider. I laugh at the spectacle.

* * *

I drive away and can't help but reminisce back to Dollicia. I met her at Maestro's Steak House on Canon Drive in Beverly Hills one night. We kept exchanging glances from across the table where Jay had introduced us. As they were leaving, I stepped up to the plate, bought her a rose from the lady peddling them outside, and offered her my services with it as she boarded the white, stretch limo with her entourage of equally gorgeous hotties.

I almost fell completely in Love with her. She could give the most passionate kisses of any woman I have ever had the good graces to meet lips with. I used to go out with her every now and then, wondering how she got all her wealth. She eventually confided that her husband had recently passed away and left her to her own devices with his estate.

She previously lived in Mexico City, where she still had a mansion worth over six million, five cars, separate beachfront property, an organic farm in Cali, a condo overlooking Miami, and bodyguards to boot.

She was forced to move to LA because of the daily kid-nappings taking place directly in her neighborhood. They lived in a gated community, but once they exited it, there was no stopping the crimes from happening. I almost did-n't believe her until she showed me pictures of the place, and I flew there for a week to chill out. I had a housekeeper and a personal chef at my disposal. It was heaven.

When I got back, I started to hang out with her kids and learn Spanish. They were better educated than I was from the private schools down there, and they were beautiful too. It was the only time I have ever witnessed actual Hollywood agents coming up to me in the Beverly Center to ask, "Are these your kids, because they are so beautiful. I would Love it if you could bring them by my office and do a reading on camera."

I took her son skateboarding in Santa Monica and to a few "guy" movies at The Grove. I rode bikes and played soccer with her daughters. I fell in Love with them. They brought the kid in me out again. Made me feel youthful and alive just like today with Bobby.

In the end, it turned out to be stagnant waters because the FBI were watching Dollicia's every move. She finally confessed that her former Anglo-Saxon, American husband was involved in the highest echelon of the cocaine drug cartel, and was rubbed out by his jealous lover, Eva, in order for her to get her share of the goods. What a mess, a Latino soap opera to the nth degree!

The ironic thing is that when I first met Dollicia, I inquisitively asked, "Why in all places in the US, would you move to Beverly Hills when you could live like a queen anywhere else?" She only moved there because Eva had talked her into it for her own machinations. Later on, Dollicia was forced to relocate for fear of assassination by the other drug lord s' thugs who were taking over his old domain.

The FBI moved them and put her in witness protection. I had one night of romance with her, the night before she left. It was very special, but that was the last time I saw her or ever heard from her again. Oh well, you win some you lose some, I guess.

Today, Bobby and Michelle reminded me of that whole scenario. I just don't need to relive that feeling all over again, even though it was a fun time in my Life. I had to let it go, but it broke my heart to do it with the kids. Please spare me, God, spare me. I moved away from LA to escape this kind of drama. The last thing I need is for it to follow me here and bite me in the ass. Lord have mercy.

The Dinner
and the Challenge

I am hesitant as I wait out front of Calista's house. I feel like I am in a trap, and it is my own fault. I didn't have time to tell my brother the details. I am going to dinner with the woman of my dreams, but I feel like a farce. I have to regain control.

I walk up to the door and knock. No answer. I see no lights on either. I wait a moment and knock again. A second or two later, the door creaks open and it is Michelle again.

"Mommy will be out in a minute. We are watching scary movies; do you want to join us?"

"Sure."

I walk into a blackened environment while she holds my hand, and giggles at me as I trip over the steps. As soon as I enter the room, I see Bobby, and we start to exchange mock sneers until Calista comes down the staircase and interrupts the whole event in her evening dress, looking like a 50s movie star.

Her hair is carefully swirled back. She is adorned in a

tight, revealing black dress with matching gloves, hat in hand, and purse as well. Lastly, I veer down to notice her perfectly manicured feet and exquisite calves in high heels. She walks with grace and wraps a long scarf around her neck as she descends.

"Good evening, shall we?" she says with a slight English accent.

"Good evening, we shall."

She kisses them goodbye, and we're off. Not a word, just the subtext of tension filled looks. What kind, I am not sure, but you could cut them with a knife.

I open the door of her Mercedes G-wagon for her and help her step up inside. She hands me a business card of the restaurant as I pull out of the gated community. I don't say anything, even though I already know this place because my brother knows all the top chefs in the area, and this one hooks him up with lobster flown in from Maine for him to grill as he Loves to barbecue. I plug in and play some Marvin Gaye from my iPhone as we ride. I feel like a boy on his first date as if I was a teenager.

The ride is fairly short, and I park in silence and escort her to the door, when I finally think of something I actually have the nerve to say.

"You were supposed to work out."

"I did. Where were you?"

"You text me saying show up ready to eat!"

"We'll start tomorrow."

We go in, and the maitre d' shows us to a corner booth without even asking for a name, or whether we have reservations. I am impressed and beside myself. If this were LA, we would be being stalked by paparazzi by now and this quaint outing would not even take place. Her manager and publicist would forbid it, I'm sure.

The waiter shows up before we even open the menu and starts his showcase for us. Calista interrupts him halfway through, and orders three appetizers: crab cakes, tuna tartar, and calamari. Then before he can inquire, she goes on to ask for two dirty martinis, and a bottle of red and white wine. He leaves to put in the orders. I am not sure how to take this. I really feel like scolding her, so I do.

"Is this the way for you to acquire that body we are going to set goals for tonight?"

"On the contrary, sir, I think I should tell you—"

The waiter is back already, and he interrupts her to state his, "tonight's specials are" food monologue for us. She orders the linguini with a seafood cream sauce, the pan-fried sea bass, and the baked pears with cream-filled stuffing for dessert. I have to shake my head in astonishment.

"Do you eat like this every night, princess, because if you do—"

"This is why I need you—" She takes a sip of her martini as if she is teasing me, being the drama queen that she is, and continues. "I have to put on twenty to thirty pounds for the part of a lifetime, and then you have to get it off me before the Golden Globes and Oscars, capeesh?"

"Whoa, slow down. Are you serious?"

"As a heart attack."

"Yeah, well you might have one if you keep eating this way. What's the timeline?"

"We start filming in about a month or less. It will be a fast and furious, two-and-a-half-month shoot, and then I have to look like a runway model before the red carpet, because I am presenting this year."

"Ouch."

"Don't get soft on me now, cowboy. You're going to earn your keep."

"Oh, so I am just a ranch hand now, and you can do whatever Miss Thang wants? I think I'll take the steak and go home sista'."

"Hey now, easy, I will do everything you say after tonight, okay?"

"Promise?"

"I promise."

"Can I get that in writing?"

She pulls out a pen from her purse and starts writing on a napkin. I let her keep going even though I can tell she expects me to stop her. "Here smartass."

"Better a smartass than a dumbass." I hold it up to read it out loud while making up my own version. "You judiciously will give your body to me for the next six months. That should be long enough. I'll be sick of you by then."

"Maybe I should ask someone else. I'm sure the local guys would Love to—"

"Yeah, Love to—"

"What! What are you going to say?"

"Nothing," I mumble as I take a sip of water.

"Good. Can you do it?"

"It's more like can you handle it?"

"Oh, I can handle whatever you dish out, baby."

"That's what I heard."

"That's it, you're fired."

"Good, where is my steak?" I quickly jump up and go to the restroom.

When I come back the food is already coming. We gorge and exchange a glance or two as we sip our vino. Halfway through, she says something that makes me stop stuffing my face for a brief moment, and I can't quite figure out why. Then it surfaces cerebrally, and I have to ask.

"Why are you doing this?"

"It is my way of saying 'F U' to my ex."

"I seemed to have missed something here."

"My ex wouldn't green-light this film for me. He wanted to give it to that bitch he was sleeping with, but I bought the rights and got the backing before filing for divorce, and now he is pissed off because he knows it is a good project, and it will be going up against his film for the Oscar race next year, so he is determined to sabotage it. Fucker! He's such a fucking control freak that he can't—"

"Okay, okay, take three deep breaths. Trust me, I understand about exes."

"Sorry. I just get so angry."

I start to speak in a Confucian wise man's tone, "The fire you carry will burn you more than he. Bad for chi . . . No good for digestion."

She laughs, and I recall the first time I made her laugh.

"Not to beat a dead horse but who is this guy?"

She reaches into her purse and pulls out a two-day old *Hollywood Reporter*, and points to an article with a picture by it. This is what I was feeling before. That weirdness that makes the hair on your arms stand up.

She gives me a look and pauses. "He is only one of the biggest executive producers in town."

"Oh, I think I've seen him before."

"Not surprised. He knows everybody and he packages deals with all the top agencies, so he is involved with almost every big name in town by only a few degrees of separation."

"I think, I saw him at the funeral?"

"Whose?"

"Mr. Luigi's, and his family."

"Oh yeah, I heard about that. Sad, very sad, yeah, he was probably there, I'm sure. If he was though it was purely for business PR purposes. The guy doesn't really have a heart, trust me on that one, anyway, how's your steak?"

"Absolutely delicious."

I drop her off at the front door, give her a quick friendly hug, and leave. Of course, I curiously desire to kiss her, but I am completely against it because I sincerely adhere to the philosophy of, "not shitting where you eat," or better yet, "don't stick your dick in the cash register."

I have begun to think of her like my sister now. My initial interests in her were purely romantic and led by infatuation at one point, but now it has become overshadowed by our business relationship and fitness endeavors.

It was an interesting night. I drive away feeling like it is a new dawn for me, but one of ambiguous uncharted territory to be explored. She has agreed to put me on salary until this is over. I never thought I would see the day when I am training one exclusive client.

This is how it should be. Personal training is not a necessity. It is a luxury. It has become a whored-out trade of burnout capacity and quantity, not quality. Now I can focus on one individual with my whole being. I will become an actual Life coach. A Fitness Guru/Master/Wizard, just watch me! She is in for a ride.

I still find myself puzzled about her ex, Tom. She wouldn't say his name the whole night for some reason. It's easier to keep it less personal, I guess. It's kind of like getting mad at a person in an inanimate object, like a car, or a killer who stops killing someone when he starts to care. Once the person makes you emotionally connected, it is much harder to be mean and ruthless.

Calista still Loves this guy whether she will admit it or not. Tom did a number on her, and now he is trying to clean up the broken pieces and take out the trash, but he may have screwed over the wrong woman. Hell hath no fury like a woman scorned! I think that's the saying, and it'll come back around to hit Tom in the ass if Calista has her way. If she had a gun, and he walked in the room at the wrong time of the month, he would be a statistic. I wonder what Bobby and Michelle think of him? I hope I never have to meet him.

Kids, Training, and Goodbye to the Rockies

"Captain Crunch, FROSTED flakes, FRUITY pebbles, FRUIT loops—how appropriate!" I blast him.

Bobby throws an empty plastic cup at me.

"This stuff is crap, Little Man. You need good, old-fashioned oatmeal to give those muscles energy!"

Michelle nods her head yes, as she says, "I like oatmeal." She is the golden child.

"Oatmeal sucks!" Bobby is the tyrant.

"Whatever. I bet I can outrun you when I eat oatmeal, but if I don't, I bet you're faster than me."

"Uh-uh," Bobby fires back in disbelief.

"Let's try it. I'll eat oatmeal with Michelle today, and we'll race up the driveway after. Then tomorrow you'll eat oatmeal, and I'll eat Fruity Pebbles, and we'll race after and see who wins. If I lose the bet, I'll take you and Michelle to the movies, horseback riding, or whatever you want. What do you say, Little Man?"

He growls, "You got a deal, sucker!"

"Alright, Michelle will be the judge. Let's eat."

We eat like we are starving and in anticipation. The contest has already started. Bobby sneers at me the whole time while gobbling up the entire contents of his bowl. I finish, and Michelle barely puts a dent in hers, but has the biggest toothless grin on her face as she waits for the main event. Finally, I speak up.

"Are you ready?"

"It's on, bring it!"

We go outside and walk to the bottom of the driveway. It can't be more than two hundred yards. We line up at the edge of the curb and look up to the top. Michelle already has her arm up.

She screams, "Ready, Set, Go!" as loud as her tiny lungs can project that miniature voice box, and swiftly drops her arm down.

I start off slow to let Bobby feel superior. He's such a presumptuous little brat, but whoa he's freakin' fast, and I have to punch it up a gear in order to even stay in the race. We keep neck and neck as we go through the curve, and he looks over at me and smiles that Cheshire cat-smile. I can't believe the nerve of this little shit.

Then he takes off like a bat out of hell. Damn, he's really quick! I might actually lose. It's the last half, and I really have to kick it in to pull away. I pass Michelle, and she throws her arm down again for the finish line. I am almost breathing hard and thought I was possibly toast. Bobby isn't breathing hard at all. I look at Michelle's huge grin.

"Bobby was the fastest one in his school last year."

"Really, wow, I can see that."

"I'll get you tomorrow man!"

"We'll see about that."

We go in, and Calista is eating Michelle's left-over oatmeal. "See," Michelle squeals, "Mommy likes it too."

I look directly at Calista, "That's good, because Mommy is going to be eating a lot of that soon."

She smiles as she licks the spoon and rebelliously replies, "Yeah, but for now Mommy can eat anything she wants. Who wants to go get Krispy Creme with me?"

They both scream like banshees, and I just shake my head at the fiasco and sarcastically say, "Thanks for the backup, Mom."

"You'll get your way soon enough."

"Alrighty then, I give up. I'm going to the gym, see you guys."

"Byyye!" Michelle and Calista sing in unison as they walk out the door with Bobby.

* * *

I go to the local gym after starting the "cleanse." I will remove all the crap from the house over the next few days and replace it with healthier choices. That way, when she goes looking for that nighttime snack, or craving to fill those midday munchies, there will be nothing that can hinder her progress. I just take it out of the equation altogether.

I walk in the building, and the whole place smells like chlorine from the pool area. I put in an application for training here two weeks ago at this gym. Oh, excuse me. They call it The Spa. A place for a guy to take his lazy ass to the steam room, the women to get facials and pedicures, while they both dump their kids at the pool or daycare.

I don't know if I'll get hired, but once again my bro put in a good word for me, and introduced me to Denise, the Fitness Supervisor. Denise is sweet but sort of manly. She is one of those people that live here because they Love the outdoors and train for duathlons, triathlons, cross-country skiing, mountain climbing, whitewater kayaking, etc. She could put me to shame in any kind of race, I'm sure. I respect that though.

This Spa is cool because it is so laid back, but it is actually starting to make me miss LA, I can't believe it. The difference is that people here seem averse to fitness. They only want to hire me if the doctor prescribes it because they are suffering from obesity, diabetes, high cholesterol, coronary trouble, and might not be able to see their kid's next birthday/bar mitzvah/graduation/wedding unless they change.

Getting people to do this requires major fear. Otherwise, they eat to their heart's content, sit on their gluteus maximus, and expect pampering until the sun goes down. People in LA may be narcissistic as hell, but at least they will get off their butt and do something about it before their arteries start to harden, or they need angioplasty just to stay above the ground a couple of years longer.

I think the colder weather may breed this. You just don't see it in as much totality in warmer climates like Miami, Phoenix, Cali, or even when you go abroad to some tropical environment. It is the fact that the colder it is, the more clothes you have to wear, and the insecurity you may have of being more naked.

* * *

Denise is here and looking like a cornerback for the NFL. She glides over, reaches out her hand and starts, "Hi, how are you this morning?"

"Fine, so do you think I will be able to help you out around here?" I ask.

"I think you are very well qualified, but unfortunately we are so underworked as it is, I don't know if it is worth it for you to work for us. I will hire you, but I can't guarantee that you will get much employment as a trainer for the remainder of the summer. You can supplement hours by working as a chaperone with the children's classes because you're CPR and first aid certified, but the amount of training hours purchased here on out are usually very low."

"That's okay, I get along with children. I am only looking to train a few people at this facility anyway."

"Cool, then you're hired, and you can start tomorrow. How is that?"

"That's great, thank you."

I guess I can't escape it completely. I guess it's my dharma. I guess when God called out for the blessed gifts of mankind to be dispersed among the living, I was picked to be forever a trainer.

I am back in the game but in a new locale. I am dumbfounded as well. I must have a gift. Why else would it be so easy? Isn't it supposed to be easy when you find your true calling? That's what they say.

Maybe I just need to accept it and let go of those visions of grandeur that have been seeping into my cranium like a bad bacteria poisoning my ability to absorb my real destiny, and not the illusion of an imagined one.

It could be worse. People in other parts of the globe right now are suffering and dying from starvation, natural disasters, diseases, genocide, medical poverty, war, terrorism, etc. Maybe I did that in my past Life? Why is it I yearn for more, even though I have all the things needed to survive and live very comfortably while others struggle just to stay alive?

I feel saddened by my own lack of gratitude sometimes. Is it just a natural human "grass is greener" effect that we are all guilty of, or am I just an egotistical bastard who is

sinfully consumed with my own pitiful personal concerns? I will find out too soon, I'm sure, too soon.

I look at the schedule from the local gym I just left from
and it is pretty basic and dull. I start to laugh because the
classes I used to make fun of back in Cali, like "Astro Rev,"
(which is described as, and I quote, "It is intended to align
your movements with movements of the solar system.
Each class begins with an astrology reading for the day
followed by an intense, energetic, and fun Rev session,
and finishes with astrological insight for tomorrow. Know
what's happened, what's happening, and will happen
while getting the workout the universe intended you to
have,") or "Booty Ballet Class," or "Striptease Class," or
fifty kinds of Yoga. Give me a break, *Only in LA*. Now it
makes me laugh though whereas before it made me
cringe. That's Hollywood. At least it's entertaining, and I
am starting to miss it. I think . . .

* * *

I come to my new place of employment ready to make
heads spin with my West Coast Fitness Mecca abilities,
and Denise introduces me to my new Coloradoan client. It
is a woman named Thelma. Thelma has a "slight weight
problem," Denise says. Yeah right! Thelma weighs at least
one hundred seventy-five to two hundred at approxi-
mately five-foot-two!

I am not used to this. I try to keep my composure and
maintain a pleasant smile on my face as I shake her hand.
I must maintain compassion. Yes, compassion is my new
friend. Wow, this is going to be a project, and I thought LA
clients were such a struggle?

She has never worked out, and her heart rate skyrock-
ets if she just runs to the car because someone tells her that,

"Today on Oprah we will be talking about dietary guidelines and emotional eating disorders." Okay, cheap shot.

I put her through a tortoise paced workout of unbelievable ease, kissing up to her all the while and then let her go on her merry way.

She is only half to blame as I find out she has thyroid deficiencies, and an inoperable vagus nerve. For those of you that are not that educated in this department, the thyroid affects metabolism, which in turn affects body heat and calories burned. The vagus nerve is the actual nerve that carries a signal to your brain after eating for ten to fifteen minutes. This signal, depending on how much your stomach is stretched out by those portions you consume every meal, is what lets you know that you are full, and you should stop stuffing your face.

Other than that, she is guilty of being the spoiled daughter of a wealthy father who created an internet app, and has to be one of the top one hundred wealthiest people in the world, so what are you gonna do? Do your damn job, that's what.

I promise her that if she follows exactly what I tell her, she can drop six percent body fat in twelve weeks or her money back. She could care less about the money but is very excited.

I also follow that with, "In a year's time which sounds like a long time to be this disciplined, but really isn't if you want to look good for the rest of your Life, you can lose at this twelve week rate, twenty-five percent body fat, which means you'll be a skinny girl!"

She starts to jump up and down which really means a lot of jiggling and not much liftoff. I give her thick torso a hug, and off she goes with a twinkle in her eye. Okay, maybe this isn't so bad.

Next is a newbie I met while watching the kids on a shift at the kiddie pool one Sunday evening to help out Denise. His name is Bernard.

Bernard is bored. I could tell, even though he has the personality of cardboard, or soft cheese. He is so smart, and so rich, and so freakin' lonely. I just asked him a simple question, "How is your weekend going?"

He started to blabber nonstop, like a broken faucet running over at the mouth. After a twenty-minute stream of consciousness, he finally inquired if this was all I do, and of course, I told him my training background. He promptly told me he would like to hire my services as soon as I was available. It was the easiest client I have ever gotten.

Back in the day when I used to train in a visually open, sixty-thousand-square-foot gym in Portland, Oregon, people would watch me for weeks and compare my intense focus to other trainers, and then schedule a meeting with me. It would always come out when seeing them that they were planning to interview at least three to five more trainers before deciding which one to use. To my surprise, and benefit, I can say I usually got the business, but I have never had a sale this simple.

I think Bernard is just like I was after my breakup with Wendy, and he just needs someone who will hear him out. He needs to find a positive outlet for his emotions and pain, or he will go inward with it by doing destructive things. I think inward is great if it is meditation, otherwise it will kill you.

I give him the basics, and stretch him, as he is a ball of tension right now. Poor guy. Can't say I don't empathize with him.

I train these two clients three to four times a week while trying to get my slobbish-self back to hard as nails normality.

* * *

I have been ignoring Calista a bit because she is on a three thousand calorie diet and doesn't need much attention. I still have her do a little cardio on her own to keep her body's fat mechanism's ability to burn fat at a doable level. That way when the time comes to shed, she will already be conditioned to do so. Otherwise, that will tack on another six to eight weeks that we will not have time for.

I hang out with her kids every now and then, when they need some attention. Everything is going smoothly until Calista lets me know that I will have to start training her on the set once they start filming next month.

I have always wanted to do this in LA because the cash is large. Anywhere from four to six grand a week depending on the Star's status and contractual negotiations, but I could never justify it because I would possibly lose all my other clients while I was gone, and most shoots only last six to eight weeks, so that leaves you with nothing after it's over unless you have some sort of backup.

Clients are divas, and don't care who you're on the set with at the time. They will seek employability elsewhere to fill the void. Better believe it, you're not that special. So, I never took the icy studio plunge, but now it's the time to do it.

The movie set is a "hurry-up-and-wait" routine. It is an unmerciful struggle because it is long hours that consist of last-minute changes, tedious waiting, time constraints, and food in your face all the while from craft services.

The film crews eat every time, like it is their last meal, and depending on the head chef's ego, he usually delivers some kick-ass chow with mucho calories. At low-level energy expenditure, this can present a challenge to my efforts.

I also find out they are shooting in upstate New York,

which means it will be colder yet, and this makes it harder for people to be motivated. I am not very excited to go farther north, and I feel I will definitely have my work cut out for me.

* * *

I say goodbye to Michelle and Bobby. I have grown very fond of them both, and we have become close. They actually listen to me now, and I have become sort of a cool male authority figure in their lives. I have spent more time just having fun with them than with Calista, who I have only spoke to in passing, or on the phone occasionally.

I am dropping them off at the airport with the nanny who flew here a week ago to help clean up, escort them back to LA to be taken care of, and get some homeschooling.

Okay, maybe I am just their chaperone and am fooling myself into thinking these attention deficit hellions will even miss me for a second, but Michelle hugs me. Then she whispers, "I Love you," in my ear.

Bobby punches me when I go to give him a hug good bye, in order to not appear girly or even look like he is potentially saddened at all, so I resort to a fist bump and a, "Later, dude."

I have already said goodbye to my other two newest clients and my brother as well. I am on another flight to New York. Calista and I will rendezvous in two days on the set and the fun will begin.

Lately, she looks like a model for Jenny Craig or that heavier set line of clothes for women. I hope she is ready to sweat because it is going to take some real work to bring her back to her idea of fine-dom. She has even gained more weight than necessary. The only reason I can come up with is that the movie production keeps getting bombarded with impediments by Tom. Stress makes people eat more if it already is, or becomes, an emotional venting outlet. She is bitchy and harder to deal with too. We shall see soon enough if she can walk the talk. Time will tell.

Meanwhile, I have received a few phone calls from my friend John the bodyguard back in LA, he says there is a warrant out for my arrest. Those freakin' cops decided I was an accomplice because I had not cooperated, so they had me subpoenaed just like they said they would. I didn't appear, so now I am wanted.

He also told me that while on a gig for someone, he overheard my name being linked to a hired hit. On the street, my Life is only worth five g's as it turns out. John says if I come back, he will watch my back, but it is not safe and to be careful. Great, just great, he also tells me the hit is local, so it is *Only in LA* that I have to worry about it. Wouldn't you know it!

* * *

They fly me first class to the big apple. It's in my contract. I faxed it to my sporadic client, Ryan, back in LA. He was impressed to say the least and gave me the green light to proceed, and said he wanted to put me on an annual salary when I got back, and that he didn't know why he hadn't done it already. Yeah right, what a line of BS.

In LA, you're nothing until you prove it and then when you do, everyone wants a piece of you. I, of course, said yes if he throws in a pension plan and reps me legally for free when I get back, and he agreed.

I arrive, and it is overcast. I get my luggage and arrive at the Four Seasons in NYC. I am being put up in style for a few days until shooting starts Monday. I want to see how the top 10 percent lives when they travel.

I Love to travel, but seldom get to in this line of work, although a client took me to train and coach them before the Honolulu marathon for a week and a half once. I also got to go to Australia for two weeks once. Sydney was fun and snorkeling off the Great Barrier Reef was awesome. Every now and then, one of my international banking and financier clients will fly me to Big Bear in California to train him on the weekends before ski season. I hate flying on those small twin-engine planes though, bumpy as hell, so they remind me of the Army C-141's I had to ride sideways and elbow-to-elbow in while smelling the vomit from all the guys throwing up next to me.

I check in, and the only thing that is new to me is not the bidet in the bathroom, but that the Jacuzzi style bathtubs fill up in only sixty seconds. I am quite infatuated with the novelty, as it reminds me of my childhood where I used to play for hours and become a human prune. I fill the sucker up and try to relax in the vast, porcelain bowl.

It takes a while, because I am so fascinated by the hustle and bustle of the city. It seems to have a different energy all its own that I am not used to. I have exactly thirty-six hours before I have to be at the set in upper New York State. So, after soaking my intrigue away, I order a massage, room service, and pass out in the huge king bed. Life is good.

ON THE SET

Room service wakes me up with coffee and eggs bene-
dict at three in the morning, which I preordered the night
before. I quickly pack and jam to catch my car service to
the destination of stress.

After arriving on the set, I walk around to check it out
and Max, the director, is already tearing into a key grip and
barking at the director of photography. He won the Oscar
last year, but he sounds like a real pretentious prick. I can
tell this is going to be a fun-filled, roller coaster ride of
congenial pleasure.

When I spot her, I carefully walk up to Calista while she
is being prepped by the makeup artist for her first scene to
let her see me, and validate that I am present and ac-
counted for.

I can tell she is nervous, but she shouldn't be. She is so
talented and gifted. Genius is an abused word in Hollywood,
but her skills are up there with the best. It's not an accident
that she has been nominated three times for gold statues.

I leave the area to go set up her workout that we are
scheduled to do as soon as the sun drops, if everything
goes as planned. I am going to do the outdoor

hiking/calisthenics/boot camp thing for a while until we start filming back in town.

This is going to be a project because the producers and director could care less if Calista has any time to exercise every day, but I know it is important to her, and I have to make it work, or she will blame me come Golden Globe/Oscar time when she looks like a pufferfish and is massacred/fat-shamed by people on social media.

She has achieved her goals though, and I can't believe it is her when I see her fully dressed and in character. She is not the normal Calista anymore. Unrecognizable, but I still think she is worth dying for if you have her heart. Otherwise, she is a cannon about to go off, and you better take shelter because she'll tear through anything in her path.

I see her go to the craft services table and walk over to reprimand her. I get within arm's length, and she sees me out of the corner of her eye and shoots me a pulverizing look. I hold my ground and give her the "No, no, no" finger, and she barely backs down as if she is the undisciplined, pampered royalty she is portraying.

She gets enabled and praised so much on the set, it is almost unbelievable that I can retain any authority here at all. Only some of the cool guys on the crew give me any respect whatsoever, and I can tell she is about to rebel against me too. I can't tell if it is her, or the character she is playing because she is one of those crazy method actors, so that is the icing on the cake to deal with as well.

It's a wrap for the day at least, and I tell Calista to change and meet me over at the first trailer where the few dumbbells, tubing, and other workout gear I had them bring is stored.

She says, "I don't need this tonight, let's start tomorrow."

"Really?"

"Yeah, I don't feel like it tonight, I—"

I promptly walk away as I see the set photographer, who takes photos for continuity purposes, walking by, and stop him and ask him for his Polaroid camera. He is startled but obliges me. I walk up to Calista and take a quick snapshot with it, and immediately return the camera to him. I shake it, blow on it to accelerate the process, walk right up to Calista, and shove it in her face.

"Is this what you want to look like on the red carpet for the whole world to see?"

"Fuck you!"

"Well?"

"I'll be ready in five, asshole."

"Thank you."

* * *

We blast through the workout without saying a word to each other. I just point, and she goes through the motions like a punished little girl, and I keep thinking that this cannot be the first day on the set because if things don't improve then this is going to be the longest eight-plus weeks ever.

That's longer than the actual basic training course I had to endure in Ft. Leonardwood, Missouri, or "Ft. Misery," as I recall it was so aptly renamed among us dehydrated and exhausted privates, who flowed through the cycles of that record-breaking summer. A few guys actually died of heat stroke in their bunks at night because of the incendiary heat and humidity. I had to laugh at the absurdity of it all when they would make us keep doing push-ups on the steaming asphalt in front of the barracks because some pissant started crying, and stopped, and crumbled, just making it harder for everyone. That's the ultimate scene of peer pressure.

I tell her she did a good job as soon as she finishes her last rep of the physio ball ab exercises we are doing. I don't hear a reply, but I turn and walk away before she has a chance to. I would have ignored it anyway.

She is turning into a tyrannical witch the first week, and I don't know if I will last. In LA, I would have put up with this stuff forever and a day, but now that I have been away, I seem to have less patience and tolerance for being abused by the self-centered drama queens and self-righteous divas who, at times, took me for granted.

Yes, I am a server. I try to instill better habits and healthy routines to improve their lifestyle. I go out of my way to create a therapeutic aura and environment for them to walk into and be a better version of themselves. But why do we need a fire lit right under our feet for us to make a change? They say when the pain of not changing exceeds the pain of changing you will change. With that philosophy, pain is the catalyst. Why do we have to be in pain? Myself included . . .

* * *

I am in dreamland again, and I feel something in the room and jump up from my bed as a cold shiver runs down my spine. Nothing is there. I try to go back to sleep, but unlike any other time in my Life, I am actually getting more rest than ever.

It is so nice to not have to get up at three or four in the morning to jump start someone's day, but now only be accountable for a single two-hour requirement. I am getting a bit stir crazy, I suppose. Either that, or this place is haunted.

I am staying in an old-fashioned inn. It is all wood and it creaks. Tonight, there is a pretty hairy rainstorm, and the trees are bending and scratching the roof in the howling wind. I see flashes through the windows every ten seconds followed by loud, sonic, thunderous crashes.

I try to go back to sleep. I am almost there, and I suddenly feel a warm body crawl into the bed with me and it wakes me again. It is Calista in her pink cotton pajamas, and I wonder what the hell she is doing.

"I'm scared. I want to sleep here." She lays her head on the pillow and that is it. I look at her, surprisingly stunned for a brief second, and then turn the opposite way and doze off.

* * *

I awake to be the only body in the bed. It is midmorning, and I decide to go for a jog after a monstrous cup of coffee, a tiny glass of grapefruit juice, and an aspirin to help kick-start the fat-burning process. I know all the tricks.

I am jogging by the set, and the line producer abruptly stops me and says, "Did you do something to provoke Calista yesterday?"

"What?"

"She just seems different, and we are all concerned about her."

"Are you trying to start something, or are you so self-indulgent that you have to be the center of attention?" I start running again.

"Wait a minute!" he yells.

I keep going. I believe pleading the fifth is the best course of action but silence breeds contempt and dissension among the ranks. This guy is either a fag hag magnet or has had a crush on her since middle school. Bastard, he's just stirring the soup. The things people climbing the ladder in Hollywood will do to get close to the stars.

It somehow reminds me of the time Jay introduced me to an up-and-coming young actress at the premiere of the movie *S.W.A.T.* I was infatuated over this beautiful woman, and he went out of his way to make sure I met her. As soon as we were introduced, her so-called manager saw that she was attracted to me when I shook her hand.

Then he interjected with all his will and impressed upon her the urgency to mingle and be seen with all the other cast members, even though they were overwhelmingly busy getting blinded by the photographers' glaring bulbs, and there was absolutely no room for anyone to squeeze in. I just wasn't famous enough for the attention of a new starlet.

Afterward we went to Colin Farrell's room for an after party at the Chateau Marmont, and I saw her again. He was flirting with her as he went out of his way to do with most of the girls, but she kept glancing at me, making eye contact, as if to say, "Get me out of here. Get me away from this fakeness. Get me away from this desperation."

Then she got whisked away again and from that moment on she was trapped. Stuck in the Hollywood system. Trapped in the illusionism until the lines of reality became muddled, and even she started to lose sense of what was what.

The focus of stardom is to always be seen in the spotlight and to obtain it at any cost, even if it means throwing the next guy under the bus in order to replace his or her good graces, with their projected false, illusory intention of wellbeing. Some people, like that slimy line producer, emulate the stars a little too closely by trying to find that spotlight. Imitation is the sincerest form of flattery, until it becomes a sickness.

ON THE SET: TIMOTHY AND CALISTA

OCTOBER 1

Life on a movie set is strange to say the least. It is like being adopted into a short-term family. The family can be very dysfunctional or become close-knit. More often than not, you make friends and have a good time for the most part, but when it's over, you go your own way and usually never to see them again, regardless of how well you all bonded and enjoyed each other. This is my experience anyway, because I seem to get along with mostly everyone and expect to have a good time while I'm anywhere socially. If not, then what's the point? The downside is it can be a little depressing afterwards.

The crane with the Panavision camera and the Dutch DP (director of photography) is about twenty feet in the air above Calista and her costar, Timothy, sitting under a huge, sprawling weeping willow tree.

Mr. Bugout, the director, is off to the side hissing instructions at them like a Vegas showgirl coach.

"Okay, now remember the first schoolyard crush you had and wanted to kiss."

How elementary, and he went to NYU for that? They are having an old-fashioned picnic and frolic in the forest as they have fallen in "Movie Love."

The lead actor is really cool, though. He is not so famous since he is British and been recently recruited from their grand theater scene. The word is that he Loves to play practical jokes and share a pint or two. No one here appears relaxed enough with themselves or seems to have a good enough sense of humor for any such jokes, but we are going to pull one off sooner or later.

Timothy asked me a few questions yesterday about health and fitness. He was checking me out, I guess. I offered him a free workout to put my money where my mouth is. "Actions speak louder than words," is so true in this case, but Calista is pulling a power trip and says, "No." I am exclusive to her, whereas two days ago she didn't care at all. Now that they are going to be fighting in the scenes, she is being a hard-ass, and I am prohibited from training him. No wonder why they call it drama.

I still hang out with him after they wrap for the day sometimes. She seems furious, even though she hates all men right now, and I am taking the brunt of her passive-aggressive behavior just because I am a male. She is acting so mental.

She has lost ten pounds already though and is starting to look more like her former self, but we only have a little over a month to get the rest off. The irony is that the woman in the screenplay gets thinner as it unfolds, so it makes it easier to capitalize on her method acting momentum, regardless of the hateful gender bias I am experiencing.

By the end of the film, she is supposed to be a new, liberated woman, so I have to wonder if she'll fire me on the last day of shooting if she is still in character? Just joking.

Hardly any movies are ever shot in chronological order, but they are doing it as much as possible with this one for her, for enhancing transformation and performance purposes.

* * *

The sun is setting on this day and there aren't any more night scenes left to shoot. It is time for me to put her through another workout. Tonight, we are going to do a boxing workout to get out all of that pent up animosity she has been carrying around. Women Love to hit things, too.

"C'mon, you hit like a girl!" I tell her.

"I am a girl, or did you forget?"

"Whatever."

"Don't you whatever me—"

"Watch it. You still have another thirty minutes. I can get you back."

"You're so mean."

"Stop or you're going to give me a complex, now give me some push-ups."

"I hate you."

"I love you, too, straighten your back, stick your butt out, good keep going. Okay, now let's jump some rope."

"Now I really hate you!"

"C'mon, you'll thank me later."

She is starting to really shape up, but the old confidence is lagging. Kind of like a guy who gets musclebound, but still has a mental view of a skinny, wimpy guy, or an ugly duckling that becomes a swan, and still thinks she is the former. She'll snap out of it sooner or later I hope, or she'll never be the same Calista I became so enamored over initially.

"Stop. Good job, you rocked, great workout, finally you are showing me some intensity—"

"Kiss my ass."

"Be careful what you wish for."

"Very funny."

"No, seriously, you are looking great, keep up the good work, girl."

"The director wants me to go out to dinner with the other producers tomorrow night in the city. Can I have a piece of cheesecake for dessert? I am dying for one, pleeease?!"

"Sure, go ahead, but when that day comes, and you walk out on stage in front of millions of viewers and appear in all those trashy gossip mags after, don't come cryin' to me if you look like Miss Piggy and—"

"You suck!"

"That's my line. You stole my line. Hey, it's just for another month, or two, or three . . ."

"See you tomorrow, don't talk to me until then," she scowls.

"Bye." I Love this job sometimes.

* * *

It is an overcast day with sprinkles of rain here and there. I Love it, but Max is pissed off and taking it out on everyone because it is messing up the shooting schedule when he had just gotten caught up with it.

I casually stroll over to Timothy and propose a hoax. He one-ups me and suggests a larger scheme. I am hesitant but can't help myself from enabling him to deliver. The crew is forced to take an early lunch and we have extra time to set up our blueprint of horror. This must be how *Punk'd* got started?

I am impressed with Timothy's cleverness and ole English guts to give it a go. I found out he served in the British Royal Army as a captain and led troops in battle. He was awarded a few distinct medals before being honorably discharged. This must be why he sees the men's attitudes on the set, and naturally wants to alleviate the tension and raise morale. To him it is not worth it to be so uptight when no one is dying, and nobody's Life is at stake.

We finish first while everyone is devouring the chef's special of Halibut and fresh striped sea bass from the New England waters. It was supposed to be for dinner, but he decided to boost spirits by giving us an unprecedented afternoon meal. Chef Howard is also famous for the best homemade clam chowder on the east coast, and we have not been blessed with this mouthwatering gift of cuisine since we last had it during the first week of the shoot. I guess it won some kind of food award back in the day.

During the process of setting up the serving tables, which Timothy and I so gallantly volunteered for, we were able to, most diligently, place a couple of fake mice we found in the props trailer in the soup can. We know how much the director and the line producer Love to slurp up the delicious delicacy on these dreary, cold, dark days, and sit together while they crucify the rest of us for our shortcomings with their holier-than-thou astounding attitudes.

Of course, we let all the others know that the soup is off limits, and only for exclusive personnel that day due to the limited supply and add a wink as they enter the chow line, and we help serve them.

The lunch has been served, and we are all munching on some seriously great food and immersed in friendly tableside conversations, when there is a scream and a loud thud. This is quickly followed by a "No, no . . ." and a chair crashing as it topples over.

I look in that direction and see the line producer is laid out cold on the floor, and Max is standing up and backing away from the table as if he has just witnessed the grim reaper himself in his bowl.

It is high drama at its best, and the place is painfully silent until Timothy stands up from his seat and swiftly walks to their trays and lifts the rather small rodents out of the two bowls by the tails. He then takes the prop, nonchalantly wipes it off, and proceeds to bounce it off the table to show it is rubber and starts to crack up in hysterics. I follow his lead in an outward display of knee-slapping antics, and in the shake of a lamb's tail the whole place starts to bust up.

The joke was not on them but in the cherished chowder they so selfishly hoarded. The chef even starts to laugh after he catches on to the fact that the joke was a premeditated setup to get the two zealous, comedic, career-started, straight men back for all their lack of a sense of humor, and their ridiculous, ball-busting demeanor during the shoot.

Someone screams, "Medic!" and an on-site paramedic comes over and puts a cracked open ammonia capsule under his nose to wake up the fainted line producer. He comes to immediately, and we stop laughing except for a couple of late chuckles. Timothy stands there in all his bravado and starts clapping to show he is giving them a hand for being such sports and the butt of such a horrendous prank. Everyone joins in. He continues to smooth things over, and we all go back to our previous chitchat.

The line producer excuses himself and goes to leave the room. I intercept him by the restroom as he walks out from taking care of business.

"Are you alright? Thought we lost you there."

"I'm . . . I'm afraid of rats and mice. Childhood thing."

"Really? Sorry about that. I'm afraid of two-faced pricks and scheming liars. Childhood thing."

"Touché, bitch."
I pat him on the back and walk back to the lunchroom.

* * *

The weather has cleared up, and the sun is peering through the sky's ceiling, casting shadows on the frost-covered town. I go to Calista's room and knock on her door. No answer. I knock again and I hear a faint, "Come in."

I walk in, and she is sitting in a chair in her workout clothes just staring into space at the wall.

"Are you ready?"

"Yeah . . ."

"That sounds inspirational." Silence. I walk up and lightly massage her traps and shoulders. "Is everything okay?"

"I feel like shit. I look like shit. I can't stand it! Will I be ready in time?"

"Yes, you will, but if you just sit here, you won't."

"I have never felt so ugly and fat."

"You can sit here and sulk, or you can do something about it."

"Don't lecture me with that positive thinking psycho-babble."

"Well, what do you want me to say? You're right, and you should just give up? Look, this was your idea, and I told you it would be a challenge. You are still on course, and don't forget why you took on this project in the first place. We set a goal, and we will get there. Just because you're having doubts is no reason to start a pity party. Get your ass up, and stick to your guns. Show him how strong you are by finishing this. Isn't this your ticket to prove you got the goods, and blow the critics away who thought Tom was pulling strings for you all along? Let's make them eat that bullshit!" She puts her face in her hands and leans over in the chair. And I thought my pep talk was going so well.

"Hey, hey, what is this?" I kneel in front of her and pull her hands away from her face. Two tears roll down her cheeks, and she looks at me with that look. The look of a person who has tried to be strong so long that the walls in front of her emotions that have been her fortress are now crumbling down in her time of weakness. She is starting to question whether it is all worth it. Whether it really means anything anymore. Whether she has the strength to fight another battle in the war of Life.

"Do it for Michelle and Bobby. They are all alone right now, missing you and it has to be for a reason. They Love you and believe in you, and you're all they got, so do it for them!"

"I'm over it, let's go," she sniffles as she wipes her face off, stands up, and gives me a hug, and whispers in my ear, "You're awesome."

* * *

It is the last day of shooting, and Timothy pulls me to the side and tells me he was supposed to take his daughter to the Gwen Stefani concert at Madison Square Garden for her birthday, but she became very ill and is unable to fly, so he is taking a red-eye to London tonight and wants to give me the tickets to take someone, maybe Calista, on behalf of him and his daughter, who happens to be the same age as Michelle.

I laugh when he tells me this, "I'm not falling for this one."

"Truly, I am not mad. Look, I have the tickets." He puts them in my hand. "Take her."

"No, I can't. It wouldn't be—"

"Bloody hell."

He walks up to Calista and starts talking to her. I watch. She smiles and gives him a hug, and he comes back.

"She would be delighted, so go with her, you fool. They are amazing seats. I want you two to enjoy them on behalf of my sick daughter!"

"Well, since you put it that way."

"But you have to mail her a T-shirt."

"There's always a catch."

"Doesn't matter. Calista's daughter's favorite is this Gwen lady too, so kill two birds with one stone."

"Will do, thanks and take care."

"You too, mate," he shakes my hand, and he's off. What a great human being. I'm going to miss that guy.

THE CONCERT
AND THE KISS

DECEMBER 1

It is a bright night with the stars winking at us beside the beaming full moon as we exit the limo and walk toward the event with a gift bag from Timothy. The cool air feels good on my face as I turn and firmly grab Calista's hand to guide her up the stairs and go inside.

She looks sporty casual tonight, with her baseball cap and matching velour sweat suit that hugs her hourglass figure. Now that I have been away from the gyms in Hollywood for a while, my distorted view of fitness allows me to find a new sincere appreciation for a woman with a little meat on her bones and curves in all the right places.

She is trying to be discreet as usual, but the paradox is that when people don't notice her, she starts to become insecure since she has put on that extra weight.

We find our box seats with the help of an usher, and they are smack dab in the center with some press people and a few other VIP's, and I have to marvel about how he obtained them in the first place. I almost can't believe the view. I am not one for pics, but I have to snap one for the little girls because it is so perfect and the stage so vibrantly colored.

Calista hasn't said a word but looks over and gives me the prettiest smile I have seen since our first introduction by Jay not so long ago. I smile back like a kindergartener to his puppy-loved teacher as I momentarily reminisce about how I was scared to even look her in the eye, much less speak to her, and now she is sitting next to me.

The Black-Eyed Peas have been trying to rock the house with their four-hour encore song "Let's Get It Started" and Calista is sipping champagne and giving me the third degree about what else is in the bag that I pulled the bottle out of.

I just smile and point to the stage with a surprised expression to distract her as if she is missing something amazing. It happens to be a piece of NY cheesecake I acquired for her from Maria's before she checked out of the Four Seasons. The concierge hooked me up. It is a surprise.

I reach in the bag and find it. She catches on to my false distraction and becomes quickly attentive to my efforts to be discreet.

"Now close your eyes." She gives me an impatient little girl face and stamps her feet in an anxious pitter-patter. "Just do it, and no peeking!"

She does, and I open the container and scoop out a huge scrumptious bite with the plastic fork. "Keep them closed. Now open your mouth."

I place the bite on her tongue. "Oh my God! Oh my God! That is better than sex . . .Well, I'm not so sure about that but damn!"

"Now, this is the only cheat you're going to get until after the big day, so take it, and I want you to cherish every single bite like it is your first and last, a'ight?"

"Yes, my lord. Whatever you say. I am at your mercy and command."

"Good answer . . . Okay, nice and slow just like gourmet sex."

"Trust me, I got it!"

The opening act is now over and was second fiddle to the dessert anyway. I refill our glasses.

"You are the man, this is sooo good. This has to be the best I have ever had. Did you get this at—you did! This is from Maria's! That's my favorite in the whole world!"

She is in food heaven and completely oblivious to anything else right now, vivaciously enchanted in oral exhilaration. She finishes a few more orgasmic-looking bites and gulps down some more champagne, and I refill the glass.

Miss Stefani just came out and started her set with some song I have never heard before. Calista slams another half glass.

"Hey slow down there, princess."

Gwen starts to belt out her first trademark song, "What-you-waiting, watch-you-waiting, watch-you-waiting, watch-you-waiting fooorrrr"

Calista stands up and starts to dance, pulling me up with her. She screams in a primal outburst of joy and puts her arms around me and pulls me into her hips and lip-synchs the chorus to me. I dance with her for a verse and the chorus starts again.

"What-you-waiting, what-you-waiting, what-you-waiting, what-you-waiting fooorrr."

She suddenly stops and looks into my eyes with this strange look as if she is sad and almost going to cry.

"Are you okay?"

She passionately grabs my head and deeply begins to kiss me. At first I hold back in complete surprise and conflicting thoughts from the way I have programmed my brain to treat her out of respect and necessity for our professional working relationship.

Then I feel her hands, breasts, and pelvis against mine. Her soft, succulent lips barely touch mine again, and I taste her breath and it is all over.

I pull away for a second, as if to regroup, and look deep into her insatiable, effervescent-blue eyes to define the moment. Then I grab her neck with one hand and the side of her cheek with the other, and start to inch towards her lips again.

I give her one last intense look to let her know that I am going to give her something real, something vital, something she will never forget, and I lip-lock her.

She grinds her hips into me even more and starts to moan. With my lips, I vehemently make my way down her neck and up to her ears, and back to her mouth with as much passion as I have in my virile body. Like it is the last thing I will ever get to do on this planet. Like it is an Olympic event, like a man. A man who is in Love.

The world seemed to stop for a moment. Everything around me became nonexistent. I was floating with an earthly angel surrendering to the satiating, ecstatic, euphoria of two souls connecting on the deepest living level.

I did not think this could ever happen to me. I thought God had handed out all of the remaining lottery tickets for Love, and I missed the second round of the giveaway.

It seemed like forever, but must have only been seconds before we stopped, looked at each other and started again, but were forced to stop as we started to fall over in the box and topple into the seats next to us. We knew that there was no turning back. We smiled at each other and understood. She reached for my hand and held it for the rest of the concert while I watched and she danced like a teenager.

* * *

The red-eye flight to LA is catching some turbulence, but Calista is crashed, and her head is resting on my shoulder. She used up all her energy at the concert. We got the shirts, and I called Timothy and thanked him for it. He was happy because his daughter was feeling better. I can't sleep for shit on airplanes and tonight is no exception.

I start to recollect everything I left back in LA and how strange it will be to see everyone again. It seems like I have been away forever. I wonder if I have changed, or if my old clients will be back? How they are doing, and whether they are mad at me for bolting so unexpectedly, even though they had commitments themselves, and I needed to recover from the accident. Will my supposed "friends" still be in the game? Will Jay still be hustling?

I called Cindy, and my place is still safe and sound. John is looking out for me. I have to go to the police, eventually, and clear that up. I feel like I am sort of starting over with a new lease on Life, but will I be able to keep it up like I used to. The same hours, the grind, the motivation and energy required to kick-ass? Do I have a choice?

How will the Calista factor play out in Hollywood? It won't be so easy. The press will not be that kind. They will follow her everywhere, and the anonymity we had in Colorado will be nonexistent. Will she even want me around when we touch down? Who knows?

* * *

The black Lincoln town car and driver meets us at the luggage pickup. Calista passes out in the car before we even get out of the airport. I sit half awake and groggy in silence on the way home. He drops me off first, without even asking for my address, and I assume that it must be premeditated. I get out and walk away when I hear the window lower behind me.

"Devon." I look back. "Can we train next Monday morning?"

"Of course, princess. Meet me at the stairs at ten."

"Okay."

I pause for any remaining connection. None. The window goes back up. She's tired, and so am I.

Cin and the
Calista Reunion

December 9

Today is the first day of the rest of my Life. I abruptly
wake to Cindy jumping on my bed at six in the morning.
"D, you're baaaaaaaacccccck!"

For a moment before my consciousness regains clarity,
I actually believe that I happened to arrive back in LA on
the exact date of a seven-point-five earthquake we've been
escaping for a while. At least until I clearly see Cin's boobs
bouncing up and down in front of my face.

If I remember correctly, this chick never even had a
thought pass through her head before noon, much less get
up before the sun came up.

"Hey, hey, calm down."

She stops, falls on me, and hugs me as if I was Santa
Claus. "I missed you so much."

"I missed you, too."

"Let's go have breakfast at the Griddle!"

"Sure, give me twenty and I'll be ready."

"Yyaaaaaaaaaayyyyyyy!"

I drag my ass out of bed and get dressed.

* * *

We are at the Griddle on Sunset, and it is packed as usual. Once again, we argue over sharing. Why is it girls like to share food so much? I used to think it reflects the bill, but the trainer in me has discovered it is really the quantity.

Girls feel less guilty if they share because then they know they won't eat a whole portion of anything by themselves. The problem is that their selfish desires take over if they're H.M. (high maintenance), and then they try to make you share food you didn't even want to eat.

After deliberating for a few minutes, we agree to share a stack of whole wheat pancakes called, "Wholey Moleys."

"I am so glad you're back D. Are you going to stay?"

"Yep, I am back for good, I think."

"Well, I missed you, and I won't let you leave me like that again!"

"Okay?"

"Besides the police kept bugging me. I am tired of those guys knocking on our door when I only have a mask, and a crop top, and panties on."

"They are still coming by?"

"Si, señor."

"That's not good, do you talk to them?"

"No, it is always the same two guys, and I am sick of them."

"Good. Anyone else?"

"No. Wait! A guy did come by himself, and I talked to him through the phone when he buzzed. He said he worked for an independent consultant. He asked if you were friends of Ryan's, and I said I didn't know."

"Good girl."

"What's going on D?"

"I'm not sure Cin, I'm not sure . . ."

* * *

The sky along the beach is overcast, but it is nice to be back. I drive down the long San Vicente stretch of road through the Brentwood neighborhood where the morning joggers, bikers, and speed-walkers group together for inspiration and commonality to get their sweat on.

I turn on fourth street and park by the stairs. They were named *Shape* magazine's number one outdoor workout. I make sure that I tell my clients that right before they commit to meeting me here for a gut-busting, air-gasping cardio workout.

I am stretching a bit as she pulls up in her rarely driven, graphite-colored Porsche Cayenne turbo. She gets out and walks over. I have only been away from her for a few days, but she looks even fresher than before. She is almost at normal proportions again, and I have to admit, I am impressed. She strolls over like a supermodel with her hips, slicing the air around her while cradling a cup of coffee from Starbucks.

"Good morning, madame."

"Good morning, sailor."

"I hear you're going to be legally single soon."

"Really? Where did you hear that rumor?"

"On Extra and TMZ."

"You're kidding, right?"

"Of course."

"Whew, I know they are on top of shit, but damn! The divorce should be final this week."

"Congratulations!"

"I feel great, let's work out!"

"That's the spirit!"

We take off jogging. The vibe between us is silent and peaceful. Not much is brought to the table except the occasional "Beautiful day" or, "It's good to be back," to which the typical early morning reply while huffing and puffing is always the bland "Uh-huh," or "Yeah."

During the verbal silence, and the drumming cadence of our shoes hitting the pavement, my mind drifts and shifts back to a swift Rolodex recount of all that has happened right before, and after, I conveniently left town. So much has happened so fast that I haven't really processed it all.

In Colorado, I was forced to put what presently mattered most into perspective just to keep it together, but now I realize I haven't fully dealt with Sammy's death, my accident, saying goodbye to Wendy, being fired, and why I am even back.

I was in a sort of denial and now that I am here again, it seems to come bubbling back up in my face like volcanic lava. Denial, the word that as an acronym so aptly means: Don't Even Know I Am Lying.

Was I lying to myself? Not being true? It did happen. Somehow deep down I guess I mentally need to make sense of it all. I need to have or find more closure. A finish line, a conclusion.

Calista breaks the silence with, "C'mon, I'll race you to the stop sign for lunch!"

"You're on."

I let her win, and she loves me for it. She gives me a kiss on the cheek, and we decide to meet at the cafe down the street after I stretch her a bit. She says she has a few things to fill me in on during lunch.

As I pull out, I notice we were being watched and

photographed by someone. Damn paparazzi are already on her. If they see us together too much, I will be the new boy toy for her to rebound with, instead of just her trainer, and show up in the tabloids in many, very unflattering photos as well. Great, just what I wanted to go down in history as. Welcome back to LA.

I arrive at the place and walk to the table where she has just sat down and notice she has put on sunglasses and a hat. She looks at me and starts to talk with a sad tone in her voice, "They followed me all the way here. I have only been back one week, and they have already made us."

"We are just training."

"Yes, but that is all we can do. Listen, I think we need to take a quick, small break. I am going to do cardio at the house, and then resume training in a month with you, okay?"

I am somewhat crushed. I stupidly started to subconsciously believe this was going somewhere. What a fool I have been to think I was going to have her fall in Love with me. She was just leaning on me until she could stand on her own two feet.

"Sure, I understand. Just promise me that you will stick with the cardio frequency, and we'll pick up the conditioning as soon as you can start again."

"Somehow I knew you would understand. You're a real man, and that is so hot."

I am ready to drink liquid Drano and cut my wrists!

"Oh! I have a new client for you, but it is not to take my place. You better not put her first or I'll be soooo sad-mad."

"Really. Who?"

"It's Sheryl. You know, my friend who played my sister in my last picture?"

"Ooohhh yeah, her . . . Wow. She needs a trainer?"

"She wants to start soon, and remember she's married!"

"Now why would you say something like that?"

"I'm not worried about you. I'm just worried about her!"

"I promise to be on my best behavior, besides . . . I'm not that kind of boy."

"Yeah whatev."

A man walks hastily up to the railing on the patio where we sit, and proceeds to lift up his camera to catch us in a moment in time. I guess telescopic lenses aren't good enough anymore. He's trying to catch her pissed off and ugly. I lift up the extra menu sitting in the vacant chair next to me, and quickly open it and block his view.

The manager sees the spectacle and comes over. I pull Calista up, keeping her face covered with the menu, and ask the waiter and manager to excuse us because we will be on our way.

We smoothly exit from the underground parking lot in back, but as we pull out, I notice in the rear view that a black van has pulled up behind us and it looks like the same guy from out front in the passenger seat. They are working as a team.

I step on it and speed up. The van does too, and pulls up beside us on the outside, San Vicente lane, and I cannot get away as the car in front of me is slowing to make a left-hand turn. I have to stop, and he goes by slowly, only because an LAPD motorcycle cop is turning as well from the other direction.

Calista is pissed. "Fuckers!" she says. "They almost caused you to rear-end that old lady in front of us!"

"Calm down. We're fine. Everything is fine."

"Will you take me home?"

"Sure, but you said you wanted a break—"

"I don't care what I said, just take me home!"

We pull up, and Calista looks over at me and like a frightened little girl says "No one is here right now. Come inside and hold me. I want to feel safe in your arms. I am not sure when I will be able to feel that way or see you again."

What can you do? "Okay . . ."

We get out, and I am getting that tingling feeling like the first time I lost my virginity. Like you don't believe it is happening, but it is. Like you're so excited but nervous at the same time.

I shut the front door and turn around to say something, and as I start to mouth the words, I am met by the full force of her body pressing against mine, and her hands start to rip off my shirt.

I always envisioned this moment to be purely a romantic encounter, or an exotic getaway, but it has evolved into a visceral, impetuous, heat of the moment kind of thing. I am now going into uncharted territory, believe it or not. I have never slept with a client before and have always said I never would.

There is an exception to every rule and rules are made to be broken, but I am not sure if this is a good—she starts to undo my pants. I put my hand between her legs, and she starts to moan in my ear as she bites my neck. It's all over. There is no turning back now.

She starts to go south with her supple lips on my abs, but I stop her and pick her up. I carry her in my arms up the stairs to the master bedroom and literally throw her on the bed.

She pulls me down on top of her. I kiss her on her chest, and navel, and inner thigh, and knees, and start to pull off the rest of her clothes. There she is before me, in all her naked glory and completely captivating. I stop for a split second to admire and relish the view. Calista rolls over showing me the whole package, and I am in motion again. This is the last freeze-frame moment I remember.

The rest is like an obscure, erotic, surreal dream. Our bodies entwined in an intense, enraptured embrace, like I have never known before. Once again time seemed to stop. We were floating in a bed in the middle of the Universe as if nothing else existed. All of LA could have fallen into a sinkhole, and we wouldn't have noticed. It was passion at its best. It was sensuous. It was pure.

Back in the
Saddle Again

December 23

I'm driving down Hollywood boulevard and feeling cryptically hypnotized by the parallel column of palm trees on each side of the corridor of road.

It has been a fast two weeks since my last magical moment with Cali, and although she hasn't called me once, or returned my only phone call, I can't quit thinking about her. Yep, I've been annoyingly shot again by the lurid Cupid. He got me twice. It was bad enough the first time. I know, be careful what you wish for.

I am headed to the penthouse of the Fountain Towers to train one of my new clients. Businesswise, things have been rolling like clockwork since I got back. No red tape worries either, except for that pesky warrant I seem to keep avoiding.

I pull up, and the valet takes my car from me as I exit. I go up the cherry wood and glass elevator and let myself in the front door after no one answers my knock.

"Hello?" I walk through the place, and notice she is

outside lying by the pool in a bright yellow bikini with her earbuds in.

It is Sheryl, the client Cali referred to me. Her husband is on tour with the band. She loves him, but it is funny how since he has been gone, she seems to want to train more often, whether we actually workout or just have lunch together on the deck.

I could care less. The view is worth it, the view of LA, and the fact that she is a freakin' ten in that swimsuit. Besides the seaweed salad, extra spicy albacore roll, fresh Toro salmon sashimi, and green tea is a major bonus too.

* * *

Afterward, she asks me to go shopping with her, and I have to regretfully decline, as I am off to train another one of my new clients. She escorts me to the front door, gives me a hug and asks, "Have you heard what happened to Cali?"

"What?"

"She was beat up by her ex, and now the court has awarded her everything, but she is afraid for her Life."

"Are you messing with me?!"

"No, honey, I just thought you should know. Cali made me promise not to tell you, but she shouldn't have because she knows I can't keep a secret."

"When?"

"Court was this morning. She called me around one."

"No. When did he beat her? "

"Right after . . . Shit!"

"After what?"

"Right after . . ."

"What? Spit it out!"

"You slept together . . . He came over right after you

left, to ask her to take him back and try to work it out and—"

"No, shit . . . "

"Yeah, but it's not your fault! Cali told me that if it hadn't had happened, she wouldn't have seen the light and refused him and—"

"Stop. Just stop. I don't want to hear anymore."

She hugs me again. "I'm so sorry."

I push her away. "I have to go." I walk out the door.

"It's not your fault! See you tomorrow?"

I am tweaked as all get-out, and reluctantly go off to the next one at the Fitness Factory on La Peer off of Santa Monica Boulevard. I cannot stop thinking about what Sheryl said even though I am about to train an important, new high-priority client for the first time. I have to focus. F'-ing focus, focus, focus . . . Shit!

* * *

I arrive a few minutes late. I hate that because it's not normal for me, and I consider it very unprofessional. He immediately walks up and shakes my hand as soon as I bust through the entrance. I tell him to get on the treadmill and warm-up for ten. He gives me a look of displeasure, but he does it.

I follow him over to the machine, get him started, and inform him he has to get into his fat-burning zone before we start, or the workout won't work and he will never obtain the body he desires.

He wants to look like a "Greek statue" for his new movie role. He is about fifteen pounds overweight and has two months tops. "Not even enough time for on-the-spot liposuction either," he previously told me.

He seems too willing to pay for the easy way out.

Money buys you convenience and just about anything these days. It definitely will get you better health care in this country. Hell, even if health insurance pays 80 per cent, and you have to pay 20 for a new organ replacement surgery and hospital stay, you won't be able to afford to live unless you're loaded. Otherwise, it's time to pay the Pied Piper or meet the Grim Reaper.

Anyway, this guy's name is Brett. Brett is up and coming in H-town, and starting to pop up in A-list pictures and register in America's households as a name after doing a four year stint on a successful television drama. If he messes this up, his career is over.

He could retire right now with more money than most people on this spinnin' sphere will ever earn in a lifetime, but now he is trying to keep the dream rollin' and the cash pilin' up because he is a changin'. Yes, he has become a little greedier, and a whole less wiser in terms of his appreciation for the blessings he has been fortunate enough to universally receive.

Before I left town, I had become blind to this but now since I've been back, I see things differently, like I've been quickened once again by fate's chain of events to attack LA with renewed humility. Almost like when I first moved here, but without the naivety and lack of linear knowledge for the social terrain itself. I am treading less lightly in my environment from strength of character now and less insecurity as well.

Brett is starting to believe he is the characters he plays. I am going to treat him like a butter-bar 2nd lieutenant cadet in OCS (officer candidate school), and humble him. He has no idea. He thinks he is some badass because everyone puckers up to him, and there are no real physical challenges. I am going to challenge him full force.

He gets off the machine, and I make him put on the

boxing gloves and tell him to just alternate punches while I move around. Then I make him do front kicks to the kicking pad for twenty reps, each leg, followed by a set of push-ups, and crunches, and his self-imposed tough guy identity is already starting to crumble and fade.

It's going to be a long forty-five minutes for this cat. Hey, he asked for it. I believe his exact words were, "Don't be like most of these worthless trainers in this city and pussy foot around with me and waste my money. I don't have time for that!"

"How bloody insulting," as Timothy would boldly say.

We are halfway through, and I catch him eyeballing the clock, taking one too many water breaks, and any other reason to slow it down. I pretend to not be privy to his stalling techniques and patiently wait.

Right in the middle of putting on the gloves again he sees someone walking by and stops, "Tom."

"Hello, Brett, how's it goin'?"

"Great, just getting ready for my next one."

"Good, good, damn right, we got a lot riding on you, buddy!"

"I won't let you down."

"All right, you better get back to work, see ya later."

"Say hello to Calista for me."

Tom shoots him an almost disdainful, dirty look as he walks away. That was the first time I saw Brett pucker up to anyone, and the first person who didn't kiss his ass.

"That was the executive producer of my next picture. I didn't know he works out here."

"Yeah, neither did I," I want to grab the jerk by the neck and pulverize him as he slithers away, but I am still in shock. Wouldn't you know it? You hang around one asshole for an hour, and you run into bigger assholes.

He did say Calista, didn't he? I want to let Brett know how much he just put his foot in his mouth, but I am at my place of business, and it would only open me up to more questioning and potential animosity towards him if it goes awry from him saying the wrong thing again.

I'll bite my tongue, but I am scared of a lack of control where Cali is concerned. I must be in Love with her. I can't figure out why else my face is so red, feels so on fire, and I want to physically punish Tom so damn bad. I mean, I am the guy in the room that can always nonchalantly throw out that Gandhi quote, "An eye for an eye makes the whole world blind," but this seems different.

I turn it up a few more notches, and Brett is about to hurl as he doubles over. "That's it, soldier. You've earned your wings for the day. Go cooldown with a twenty minute, slight-incline walk on the treadmill, and we'll hit it again tomorrow, okay? "

"Okay . . . You're a killer."

"Please don't say that."

"What?"

"Never mind, good job, veggies and protein only tonight, see you ma ñana."

I walk away and go to see if the bastard is still around, but he must have exited the facility. I run to the parking lot where I could only be so lucky to catch him. He is nowhere in sight.

This is borderline insanity. I don't really know what I would do once I actually confronted him here anyway. Another day, another time . . .

* * *

What a day I'm having, and now I am going to see the biggest EHM on the planet. "Extreme High Maintenance" is what that stands for, and what I have renamed her in my phone as.

Cin is the less dramatic, slightly more ordinary, and original "Miss HM," but Amanda even tops her if you can believe that. I haven't seen her yet, but we spoke on the phone, and she sounded even worse than before I left.

She got another trainer to take my place but fired him as soon as I said I was back. She says, "He just doesn't communicate with me like you do," Funny, because she used a four-syllable word to imply "talk," and because I hardly ever say anything at all. I just shut up and let her do all the inevitable, verbal venting that she can. I am really her counselor. The majestic diva pays me for two things at once, so it seems, and actually saves money on regular therapy sessions.

I walk in and give her a big hug, and tell her, "Wow, you look great!" It doesn't really matter because she will counter anyway.

"You really think so? No, I gained some weight."

"Can't tell!"

"Your just being the sweetie that you are. Oh, I missed you . . ." She gives me another hug, and kiss on both cheeks.

"I missed you, too."

"I have so much to tell you!"

She gets on the treadmill, and we're off as if we never skipped a beat. "Pooky finally graduated from training school, but she is outside right now getting acquainted with her new brother. I got a new edition to the family! You have to see him. He is sooooo cute! His name is Bentley, like the car. Don't you Love it. Oh, you have to stretch me today, I am so tight and the last guy—"she frowns as if to show empathy and disgust at the same time. "He was so cute, but so dumb and he just couldn't get it together. Oh, I missed you sooo much, I am so glad your back . . . I knew you would come back. Colorado just isn't the place for you. You belong here, to us, to me! Ha, ha, Oh, I got the sexiest dress I am going to wear to the Globes, and you have to make me look good in it by then okay, sweetie? Oh, and I started a new diet I want to tell you about too, and Oh my God! I have to tell you all the dirt on the movie set in Prague!"

And it goes on and on, just like before, *Only in LA*, and I can't believe it! I actually started to forget about today's events while I forced myself to intently listen to Amanda babble about everything under the sun for over an hour.

* * *

Jason is supposed to meet me at the beach today. He has changed. I can hear it in his voice. He finished his movie and wants to show me a thing or two on the board I gave him. He says I helped him get over his biggest fear and regain control of his Life. I told him "it takes two" and that he had to "make the decision to change with conviction" regardless of my influence.

No matter. He wants to board and go to early dinner on his dime in Malibu. He says he won't take "no" for an answer. He is a man again. I Love it. This is what makes me miss LA. Did I just say that? Wow!

I park and walk up to the edge of the rocks off of P.C.H. and look out, and I see a figure in the distance wave at me. I walk down to the water as he rides one in. He picks up his board and runs over to me and says, "Hey."

"How the hell are ya?" I ask as he gives me some new-fangled handshake that I roll with.

"I'm awesome, dude, just awesome."

"As I pulled up, I saw you do that hard-carving turn on that last wave. Man, you've really gotten better."

"Yeah, I Love it. Thanks to you and my new girl."

"So, she is a keeper."

"Yeah, I proposed to her on the beach last weekend."

"Whoa, slow down, for real, daaamn!"

"Yeah, and I want you to be at the wedding as a groomsman. So whaddya say?"

"I'd be honored."

"Cool, let's go get some grub."

We go get some mahi mahi tacos, and I can't honestly put into words how amazing it is to see him better and kicking ass. It makes my heart swell. It really is good to be back.

* * *

On the way back, I stop to do some paperwork at Ryan's rolling mansion off of Coldwater Canyon in Beverly Ridge Estates.

This is where some real H-Wood players dwell in, twenty-thousand-square-foot abodes with all the basic must-have accoutrements: two pools (regular and kiddie), tennis courts (at least two), basketball court for having over a star Laker or two —and other N.B.A. B.B. players for a quick game and afternoon barbecue —a driving range and/or par three course (for that intimate brunch with Tiger Woods when he may happen to stop by), and another acre of enhanced, landscaped foliage to stroll through in some of the most expensive real estate around when you may be contemplating the meaning of Life on a boring, midday Life crisis.

He hasn't started training, but he wants me to be on retainer so I guess I can't say no to that. That means a guaranteed monthly salary amount, which I can literally bank on. Leave it to these silver-tongued lawyers though because in order to enact this benefit, I have to sign a minimal three-year contract.

This means he owns me. I am at his beck and call. Whenever he decides he needs me around, I am expected to be there. That means that if he goes to New Zealand for four weeks, and wants me to jog the beautiful plush green countryside with him at four in the morning, then I am there. It's like signing your soul over to the Devil, if you will.

I have to go through two gates to get in. As I walk from the car to the front door, John pulls up in his completely blacked out M850 BMW. I walk over to him as he gets out, and I can tell by his expression that he is happy but surprised as hell to see me. I let him speak first to see what he'll say. "Well, hello. What's up?"

"Hey, stranger. Working for Ryan now?"

"Yeah, while you were gone he hired me because he got so many death threats after the Luigi thing."

"What do you mean?"

"You know he was in bed with him, don't you? I thought of all people you would know that?"

"I guess I'm always the last to know. Sammy never said anything about business. It was more like a friendship."

"Well lucky you. I am just a hired hand around these guys, but I mentioned your name, and it helped me get the gig, so I owe you a thanks. Hope you don't mind?"

"Of course not. By the way, thanks for the heads up on the hit."

"Don't mention it, I got your back, remember that."

"Don't worry, I will. You'll be the first one I call if it comes down to that. I need to get in there and scribble some signatures." I shake his hand and give him a gangsta' hug and start to walk away.

"So, you're back for good?"

"Yeah. Let's go get some sushi and sake sometime soon, dog," I propose.

He yells as I walk away, "Tomorrow night if you're free. My treat, Katsuya. I'll call you to confirm and invite some girls."

"Do that. Sounds like a plan. See ya then."

As I reach the front door, I am greeted by the house butler and escorted to Ryan's den/office where he is obviously finishing up a conference call.

"Tell those motherfuckers if they don't take my very feasible offer, when I get done with them they won't have a pot for their fucking dog to piss in, and I will own their children's children's children as well!"

He slams down the phone and eerily smiles at me like he just pleased himself more than anyone else could ever do in this lifetime. "So, how are you?"

"I'm—"

"Well, here it is. Look it over and initial each page at the bottom, sign on the last, fill out the personal information sheet, and you can go on your merry way. Thanks for taking time out of your busy day to come by and do this, Devon." He hands me the stack of fine print.

"I think I should look this over. Can I just bring it by later this week?"

"Uh, sure but I was hoping we could finalize this today. Look, just take some time right now and skim it over. I need to go to the bathroom and grab a snack. If you have any questions, I'll answer them when I get back, okay?"

"Umm, sure."

He seems stressed as he walks out. I get up and pace for a second, not knowing whether I should become indentured to this guy. I casually flip through the stack of paper. It is at least fifteen pages of small font. I walk over to the view out of the window behind his desk.

It is the fifty-million-dollar view of nothing but

landscaped greenery. I could 't help but think that I saw much better views in Colorado, naturally, than this premeditated scenery. Of course, it is all about the location, *Only in LA* for sure. In Montana, it would be just as beautiful and one-fifteenth the price.

So, what do I do? Why am I hesitating? Have I reached the top of the line for a trainer? Is this the exalted ceiling of prosperity for my profession and is it worth it? I don't know. I exhale a huge sigh, and turn around to go sign my Life away, and as I do my eye catches hold of the smallest, fluorescent-green sticky note on Ryan's desk by the phone.

Upon closer examination, I decipher the chicken scratch as, "Larry/wk-818-750-7400, Tom/new cell #310-759-7800, Renaldo-P.I. in Co/970-366-7522, Calista hm/310-650-6574, Devon/310-739-6271." It puzzles me why my number would be on a list with these other four?

Just then, Ryan's footsteps echo from the hallway, and I sit back down and resume my reading and deciphering. I randomly thumb through to page seven and by chance notice that it says, "This contract is null and void if said party should ever fail to comply with the hereby stated rules of related client representation." In a brief, blessed moment of clarity, as I read on, I realize that I will be fired if I share any other employer that he might have business relations with. I wonder how strict he will be on this, and whether I should tell him about the Cali and Tom thing that I am partially involved in.

I look up at him and he says, "Just sign the papers, Devon. My intern put all that together. You don't have to read all that."

"Yeah, but I think you should know that—"

"What is it, I have to be at Capitol Records in twenty, so help me out here."

I, in my infinite wisdom, sign the last page, and stand up and hand him the folder. He grins that "shit-eating attorney grin" and takes the paperwork from my grasp. "Don't worry. I'll take care of you buddy, haven't I always?"

"Yeah . . ."

"Great. Thanks. See you next time." He holds out his hand and we shake.

I turn to leave, and glance at the gigantic wall of books and the few framed pictures on the middle shelves at eye level, and I spot one where Sammy is smiling and posing for a picture with Tom and Ryan. He has his hands on both of their shoulders and is in the middle between them. In the frame is a *Hollywood Reporter* cutout article with the title, "Tour de Force Productions signs five picture deal."

What the fuck! They have known each other all along. I don't know why I never knew. No one said anything, and I was never the one to ask questions about business, but they were all in bed together the whole freakin' time!

Ryan sees me pause. "Anything else?"

"No, no, just admiring the room. You know I like books. See you later."

"Bye, I'll call you to train um, starting next week, oh and I might have some extra work for you."

"Really? Okay, great."

Extra work, huh? How nondescript can he be today? This is coming from a man who makes a living using an eloquent and succinct vocabulary. What is goin' on?

I show myself to the door, and the butler meets me halfway and escorts me to the closest exit to where I parked. As I drive out the first checkpoint, past the heathenish array of exotic cars lined up along the circular drive, I start to put it all together.

Something feels terribly off. My intuition, instinct, or whatever you want to call it, is ringing off the hook, and I can't help but wonder if I haven't just been an ignorant pawn in all of this corruption between the greedy knights of the roundtable of show biz Camelot?

I need to get to that envelope again. It is time to either bury this thing and move on or get involved. Hey, I could get some hush money out of this, or I could end up digging my own grave in the desert for a dirt nap on some Vegas trip if I'm not careful. Do I play, or get played? That is the question.

* * *

It has been forever and a day since my beloved Guru Chick has towered over my helpless figure on the needle bed for an hour of Far Eastern, therapeutic, corrective medicine.

She is the enlightened voice of reason that lets me know how in need I am of fixing my unbalanced yin-yang, and that my state of being "me" is where "it" is at, but not irrelevant to what else may be going on around me in the fateful scope of destiny.

I try to find that place of peace in my somewhat chakra aligned body and breathe out nothing but visualized positive subconscious pictures of a divinely designed Life as best I can.

Still, she softly says, "Rest because I am placing a lot of pins today for an intense treatment." And I have to wonder if I will ever be farther along the enlightened path at all, or if it's just the bettering of another illusion like everything else?

I pass out in my mentally depleted weary state and flashback to my kindergarten youth. I, for some unknown reason, completely relive the time my mother picked me off the concrete after she accidentally slammed my head in the car door when I suddenly reached in to extract my momentarily forgotten painting I had made for her in class.

She just held me and cried while the crimson liquid dripped nonstop from my scalp. My dad came screeching around the corner in the dark brown, unmarked government car he drove from the army, and she carried me and held me in her lap all the way to the hospital.

It was only a gash the size of a quarter when they wiped away the blood from my forehead. Head wounds are so deceptive. I needed some stitches but from the panic, I actually thought I was going to die even though I had absolutely no concept of death at that age. I was still on my first dog and cat. This was the first time that I realized that I was actually, truly Loved.

* * *

The therapy time is up, and I am forced back to reality as she begins to pull out the pins and says, "You were out for a while and dreaming deeply. Take a few minutes and walk around the block before you drive away to regain your sense of self."

Then she does that thing, and I close my eyes and try to relax as she is once again "assessing me within." After about what seems like an eternal five minutes, she stops and smiles and says, "You are letting go of the painful shadows that clouded over your happiness, and have become open to new things. This is good, I am so happy for you. Stay open for more."

I am of course perplexed to the specifics of what the hell that really means and how much I can bank on it, but I say, "Thank you," and get dressed to go, but ponder whether the "letting go" of Wendy is the "painful shadow," or is it the Cali dilemma that I currently find myself "letting go" of?

I walk out and her next human pin cushion is waiting, so I give her a hug goodbye and discreetly ask, "What did 'more' mean when you said 'stay open for more'?"

"Oh, I just felt more shifting coming into your Life."

"Oh, okay, bye."

"Bye-bye, sweetie."

I am in a daze as I walk to the car. She was right. I need to take a walk. I can't believe I literally buy into this hocus-pocus. Somehow the ambiguity of it all hits me in a place of nonlinear, truthful, logic though, or else I wouldn't do it, I guess?

I try to drive like normal, which in LA is like playing a video game where a car can pull out in front of you, blind-side you, or overtake you at any second. Still a little out of it, as I cruise down La Brea, a man in a hat with his left turn signal veers into my lane, and I honk at him as I go around his nondriving ass.

A moment later, two LAPD cops on motorbikes pull me over to see if I've been drinking. The smaller one walks up in all his bravura, tapping his baton in his hand like he is the type who would jump at the chance to club baby seals. I tell them they got the wrong guy, and he thinks I am being a smartass and asks me to step out of the car. I refuse and he calls K-9 backup.

While waiting, he tries to scare me into letting him search the car. I tell him once again, "NO!" and after consulting his partner, as if it is a Geneva Convention violation, they reluctantly decide to let me go.

He tells me to "watch my driving," and does his best to threaten me with his eyes. This guy must be a pissed off rookie, talk about a Napoleon Complex.

On the radio station, I faintly heard the local, hip-hop DJ from 105.9 say there has been a bank robbery just down the street, and three people were shot. Both cops ran to their bikes, and broke out immediately, and it never comes up that there is a warrant out for my arrest after radioing it in ? They are desperately trying to put out fires, so I caught a lucky break, I guess. Then again, I could be a serial killer too. That's law enforcement for ya.

Blowin' Off
Steam with Jay

I am getting ready to go out. It has been quite a while, and I am looking forward to a wild night out with the month I am having. My cell rings and I answer, "Hello," before recognizing the caller.

"Devon, it's me, do you have a minute?" Cali asks me on the other side catching me by complete surprise.

"Of course, what's up?"

"I miss you."

"Yeah, well that's nice, as a matter of fact I'm getting ready to go out and—"

"I need to ask you something."

"Can you call me later this week, I have to go—"

"Devon, stop! I do! I miss you, and I want you go to the Globes with me."

I have to take a mandatory ten-second pause for this to regain my composure.

"Devon?"

"Are you sure? I mean, I don't want to get in the way, really I—"

"Devon, I want to be with you. Me and Tom are over."

"I heard."

"I'm sorry I didn't tell you. I thought you might over-react."

"Yeah, well I don't know what to say."

"Just say yes and go with me. I miss you so much, and I don't care if the whole world knows it. I Love you."

My home phone rings, and it is the front door. "I have to go."

"Devon?!"

"I'll call you tomorrow." I hang up the cell halfway in amazement and half in disbelief of what just happened. I blow it off, too good to be true.

Jay buzzes again, and I let him in. My long-lost partner in nightlife crime has come by to pick me up, take me out, indulge in excessive debauchery, and impress upon everyone as much liver-aging drunkenness, and defilement as possible.

I open the door for him, surprised that he even stepped out of the vehicle to come in. He tells me to, "Pack an overnight bag and a suit, we're going on a road trip."

"What?"

"Just do it!"

"But I have to take care of a lot of—"

"Don't be a pussy. C'mon, we need to get going!"

He always throws his weight around. The power of suggestion and/or imposed will. The last time this happened, we ended up in Victoria, Canada, and I almost didn't make it back across the border.

He is impatient, "Let's go, girl!"

"Fuck you!"

"That's the spirit!" He stole my line, too.

I finish, and we're out the door and in the elevator. It

stops on the ground floor and Cin gets in. "DEEeeeee!" She practically smothers me in Love. I watch Jay's expression as she hugs me. Other than checking out her ass, he almost starts laughing out loud, and I flip him the bird, unbeknownst to her.

"Where are you going? I want to hang out with you guys."

"Uhmmm, I don't know?" I look at Jay.

Jay quickly responds, "We are going to go to my mother's house in Orange County to talk about starting a new business."

Cin looks at Jay while he says this, and then suspiciously doubles back to me to check out my reaction. "What kind of business, D?"

Before I can even speak Jay says, "Organic yogurt shops. They're the hottest new franchise."

"That's great, I Love that stuff. I mean I Love yogurt."

The elevator door starts to shut on her as we exit. I look back at her as we run out, "See you later, Cin."

"Let's have lunch when you get back."

"Sure." The door finally shuts, and Jay stops and starts crackin' up. It is going to be one of those weekends, I fear.

"Remember my brotha', we are the party!" Jay blurts out as I jump in his new Rover. He hands me a protein bar and says, "It's good to see you," and before his phone has a chance to ring, he turns on a new NYC-remixed version of the latest 50 Cent release, and guns it.

Through my unfazed stare, I become hypnotized by the haze of the city lights as we bolt through the traffic. We are headed to the Standard Hotel downtown for a private party on the roof.

Then he says we will go to a soirée at the Playboy mansion, exclusively for the cast of a recently wrapped

Bruckheimer, blockbuster feature film due out this summer. He is threatening me with a red-eye flight to Vegas after, hence the overnight bag, but I hope he is bluffing. It is a four-day weekend, and this is how we roll, two days on, and then two days off to recuperate.

Jay's voice becomes droning background noise as he jabbers endlessly on his cell. My mind marvels and examines. I cannot believe Cali wants me to go to the Golden Globes with her as her date. They are only a few days away, and I wonder if this is just some kind of shitty stunt thought up by her prick publicist. I always have fun at such events, and normally jump at the chance to go. Why else live in Hollywood if you don't like the perks?

I can't believe I just thought that. Damn, I must like it here. Things have been good since I got back. Being an independent trainer is the only way to go. No more working for the bloodsucking gym chains. Cali was what invigorated me though and now I am a burden to her fears, and captive to her desires. What will I do? What should I do? I guess I'll figure it out over coffee Monday morning.

* * *

We are at the Playboy mansion. The other party was lame. Great views of downtown and a few cool moments, but it was mainly a drop-off for Jay. He is always working. My head must look like it is on a swivel with all the amazing, bikini-clad women running around.

Jay goes over to one of the main actors there, and I follow. He introduces me to everyone. I meet Jerry, or maybe I should say, Mr. Bruckheimer, and he is a really nice guy.

I am slightly buzzed so I go over to one of Hef's girls. She is a runner-up to Cali, but still very cute with curvaceous hips, exotic-looking, long, black hair, and electric-blue, sparkling eyes, and very friendly.

I am in heaven, but my bubble is instantly busted when I see Tom come up and say hello to Jerry. Then he turns to me, and I hold out my hand thinking I will introduce myself and tell him I work for Ryan. He gives me a look of disgust, rudely ignores my courtesy gesture, and pushes on before I can utter a word.

I want to punch him again so badly it hurts. He has it coming if it is the last thing I do. No, blow it off. Choose your battles wisely. This guy can and will crush you, especially if he knew who you are. That was stupid, but I was trying to be civil. What did I expect? This guy beat a beautiful woman. He will always be a jerk. I wouldn't have even thought of doing something so foolish if I weren't so buzzed already though.

Time to get another drink. Jay jabs me in the ribs and tells me, "We are going to the caves to go for a dip in the water with the girls." I immediately forget what just happened when two hot, blonde twins grab my arms, pull me along, and lead the way to the warm watered caverns of wonderfulness.

INCARCERATION

JANUARY 2

I am almost crawling. Every sound hurts my head. Hell, everything hurts period. I parked outside over the weekend so Cindy could have the extra spot for her girl-friends' little, powwow, pajama sleepover.

They all decided to keep me up and feed me martinis while they walked around in skimpy sleepwear with nothing else on, screeching while watching romantic girlie movies. It's a hard Life, but someone has to live it. Between that and partying with Jay, I am lucky to be alive.

I go out front to get my bags and personals still left in the car outside because I was too exhausted to carry them in. I hit the remote and start to open the trunk when I hear a faintly familiar voice behind my back. "You are under arrest. Anything you say can and will be used against you . . ." I feel the cold steel encompass my wrists as the other one slams me up against the vehicle and pulls back my arms. He pats me down while the other one finishes the "rights" monologue. I don't say a word, or even have the energy to do so. It's off to the station I go, feeling like hell.

* * *

They tell me they knew I was back in town from being pulled over a few days ago when the biker cops ran my name and plates. They say it so proudly, you'd think they'd gotten a medal for bringing me in after doing some simple police work.

I am escorted to a small room, and all I can do is think that it looks like a set on *Gotham* at Fox Studios where they interrogate and beat up the suspects. I should be worried, but I am waiting to see if they improved on their good cop, bad cop routine.

The door opens, and an unfamiliar face comes in. Another suit. He orders the two to take off the cuffs and then nonchalantly sits down in front of me.

"Hello, I am the D.A. I am working on the Luigi case, and I would appreciate it if you would cooperate, so before you even speak, I am going to make one, and only one, proposition to you. We have enough evidence to prove you are hiding evidence. Therefore, you are going to be found guilty as charged. Now if you do choose to cooperate by releasing to us that said evidence, and it results in a conviction, the charges will be dropped. Otherwise, to put it bluntly, you're fucked. So, what is it gonna be? You don't have any more time because we have reason to believe that accomplices you know will be implicated as well, so I suggest you save your own ass before the cannibals tear you apart."

"Well now that you put it that way—"

"I'm not playing games, son. You will not be protected. They will hang you out to dry."

I see the sincerity in his eyes, but I want to test him so I look directly at him, hold the stare, and smirk. "You're full of shit."

He gets up as he slams his fists on the table. "Can't you see it? You are the fall guy. You've been set up all along!"

The room is silent for a moment. He's right. "I want that promise in writing, or you can shove your proposal where the sun don't shine."

"Fine." He walks out and slams the door.

The guards take me to a small holding cell. I can't help but pace. Jail would drive me crazy. I don't know how they do it. I would hang myself. The army was bad enough when it came to control and isolation.

* * *

Here he comes. The door swings open, and he drops it in my hands. "Read each page and initial at the bottom, and sign and date the last one. The detectives and I will be back shortly to hear the candy."

I know they're helping me, but I don't have to like them. I feel like I'm ratting on my grade-school buddies.

They come back just as promised, and I tell them about the envelope and where to find it. I tell them I haven't opened it in order to cover my ass in case for this exact, potential situation. They scoff at this, but the district attorney says that it may be my only saving grace.

I even give them my keys and tell them not to scare Cin too bad when they enter the place, and they laugh at this, too. They tell me, "Get comfy because you're not going anywhere, anytime soon."

* * *

They weren't joking. A whole damn night in that finite, freezing cell! All I could do was lie in the fetal position and sleep off my exhaustion.

I am being driven home in a luxurious black and white. How comforting. Now the neighbors will chat me up for sure when I step in the elevator.

I feel a big release but am uneasy and unnerved about how this might all go down. My clients just think I've been sick for a few days. Cin called them for me. What an angel. Now I will have to go out to lunch with her or something. Damn! The cops wouldn't let me move my car, so now I have two parking tickets on the windshield.

To my surprise, at least they didn't tear the place up. They just took what they came for. When they got back, they opened the envelope in front of me for legal purposes. It contained a folder with a bunch of goodies; a list of offshore accounts, copies of drafts of large sums of money deposited for the funding of their five-picture deal, the contract for the deal, a taped phone conference call with Tom and Ryan —where Sammy and his family are threatened —printed e-mails of coercion, and more.

Sammy had dotted his i's and crossed his t's. They let me out without bail, told me to watch my back, and lay low for the next twenty-four hours, and that is what I am going to do.

THE GLOBES

I am trying to relax after the last few days when my iPhone rings. I look at the caller ID and it's Cali. I pick it up and answer, "Hey."

"I haven't heard from you. I guess that means you aren't going. I don't blame you, I—"

"Oh shit! I totally forgot."

"How could you forget? This is an important event for me—"

"Stop. I'll explain later. I do need to see you. Yes, I want to go. I have to take a shower."

"I'll have my driver come get you first. You have a nice tux?"

"Trust me, I got it covered."

"Be ready by noon."

"No problem."

"See you soon."

"Bye."

I open the closet and pull out the badass tuxedo Mr. Jones gave me from Neiman Marcus before I left town for my birthday. I never had a reason to wear it. It has been tailored for my body, and I will look like a star. I am excited and feel like a little kid. It is a nice lift after the drama I have just endured. This is going to be fun!

* * *

I am in the Lincoln Town car as it cruises through the gates of Cali's residence. I get out and go inside. As soon as I step in the door, Michelle runs up to me and gives me a huge hug. I pick her up and hold her.

"I missed you," she says.

"I missed you, too."

"Then why haven't you come around?" comes from somewhere and Bobby steps out from around the corner like a spy eavesdropping on his targets.

"I wanted to, but your Mom and I didn't know if—"

"That's bullshit!" Bobby blurts out.

"Yeah," Michelle chimes in.

"Hey, you guys take it easy. From now on, if it's okay with Mom, I will come by and hang out."

"Promise!" Michelle screams in my ear.

"When?" Bobby darts out.

"This week. We'll go to Disneyland, how's that? I've never been there."

"Cool."

"Yayyy!"

I look up and discover that Cali and her crew have been watching us the whole time. She was upstairs with her assistant, hairstylist, makeup artist, and personal fashion coordinator, a squad of men to adorn her.

She starts to slowly descend down the staircase, and I recollect the time we went to dinner in Colorado, except this time she looks like a queen out of a fairy tale. I am speechless like when we first met. She has never looked more stunning.

She gives me her hand, and I take it as if she is royalty. She says in a British accent, "I am ready for my escort."

"Yes, my lady," and I kneel and kiss her hand. The entourage from upstairs watching overhead all giggle. Even Bobby cracks a smile.

"Mommy, you look Be-a-u-tiful!" Everyone laughs after Michelle breaks down the annunciation of the word.

"You look absolutely amazing," I say to her, and then I look at Michelle and ask, "Where did the real Calista go? Who kidnapped her?" Michelle giggles some more.

"Thank you. I am so glad you're here." She gives me the lightest kiss on the lips. "And I am so bloody nervous!" she yells out.

Her assistant yells back, "Get going, you have to go!"

We walk out together and get in the car while everyone watches and waves goodbye.

On the way there, Cali doesn't say a word. She just smiles and holds my hands tightly. I can feel her hands shaking a little, but she looks so calm and poised.

Right before we get there, she turns to face me, holds both my hands in hers, looks me in the eye and says, "I feel much safer with you here. I know this isn't going to be much fun for you in the background, but it means so much to me and—"

"It's my pleasure, just do your thing and remember . . . You are the fairest one of them all."

"Devon, when I told you on the phone that I Love you, I—"

And before she can even say another word, the door opens, and the cameras start shooting. It reminds me of being on duty as a soldier in my dress greens when I had to escort a General's wife at an awards ceremony in Germany one time. I am to be seen and not heard.

* * *

The atmosphere of the Golden Globes is less serious than the Oscars. It is more of a party atmosphere, and people tend to let their hair down just a notch lower.

We make our way to the beginning of the red carpet and the interviews start. I humbly step aside to let her shine as she cannot help but do so. She is up for an award for best actress, and I am nobody, so they ignore me anyway.

I hear voices all the way in: "Is that her bodyguard?" "Who is he?" "Is that her new boyfriend?" "Where did she get him?" "Who's that?" "Where did he come from?" and "Who's the hunk?"

A few times Cali grabs me and pulls me in front of the interviewee and introduces me as her "newest boy toy," which always gets a laugh and a good response if the person is a woman or gay. I laugh it off, too. I even blush a few times.

I will be seen on *E! News*, or all of those gossip shows as that very thing, if I even make a blip on the radar. That's okay though. Most men would give anything to be just that for one night.

* * *

We finally get through the riffraff, and Cali is mingling with the other celebs. They all come up and wish her good luck. I meet everyone. I even get a few compliments on my tux from a few of her girlfriends. I am on cloud nine, Life is great. It doesn't get much better than this in my book. Not in LA.

I am contently waiting for her but in my ear, like a bad dream, I hear, "Too bad Sammy couldn't make it." It is a faint creepy whisper, but I heard it. Then, "How is he getting my sloppy seconds?" is much louder, and I spin around to see the evil voice's source. Tom is right in my face, and without hesitation I retort, "At least now she doesn't have to fake her orgasms."

Tom immediately throws a sloppy punch, which I, out of simple neural reaction can't help but duck, and he hits the person in the head behind me standing next to Cali.

At that instance, my wonder-struck Cinderella moments were over. I don't remember thinking at all. I only remember particular voices. First, the echoing voices of random people saying these hideous things about this guy named Tom, who beats women and emotionally abuses his kids; then the sounds of Cali, Bobby, and Michelle in tears; Cali's friend Sheryl the day she told me Tom hit Cali; Jay at the Playboy Mansion, laughing; and back to Tom's sinister voice, bad-mouthing Sammy's hallowed name just now . . .

They kept repeating until it was broken by the sound of crunching as my fist met his face, followed by the sound of screams, and then the sound of the endless clicking shutters of the cameras.

It takes the security a few milliseconds to respond to the ruckus. I stand their motionless, as Tom is quickly accosted and carried away in reactive protest. I am, too, but I go quietly of course.

Cali doesn't even know what happened. Tom did his drive-by verbal barrage while she was talking to Steven Spielberg. He was on his way to intercept and schmooze him up as well but couldn't resist being the King of Bullies! He just had to say something and ruin our blessed night of bliss, *Only in LA.*

* * *

Once again, I am hauled off to the station after the overly paranoid and overprotective assigned Deputy Sheriff runs my I.D.

Tom is taken in too, and he keeps threatening me as we are detained. "You're dead! Fucking Dead!" I blow him a kiss when he says this, and he goes nuts. The cops have to reprimand him and hold him down. I say nothing back, as I am still in shock.

I think I would rather be dead right now after that faux pas. Embarrassed doesn't even come close. Cali will never talk to me again. I really am dead now when it comes to this town. And everything was going so well.

The press will shred me. I will be the uncontrollable, uncivil, hotheaded Neanderthal who shouldn't have been there anyway. The quintessential fish out of water, the misfit, the guy who spooked the whole place with drama and violence in an already jumpy crowd of neurotic artistes and auteurs.

As soon as I am brought into the Beverly Hills Police Department they are waiting, the Laurel and Hardy boys, the District Attorney's henchmen. They take off the cuffs and to my surprise pat me on the back, shake my hand, and say, "Good work, kid, good work." A little redemption, I guess. "We will need a statement and then, GO HOME!"

"Yes, sir," I blurt out with gratitude. By the time I get home the awards are over, but I watch the news and find out that Cali has won her first gold statue. I am so happy for her that I feel like I am going to have to punch something else as a tear starts to well up in my eye because I won't let myself cry. Damn! What a snafu. It hurts. It really, really hurts.

I decide to go to bed before I make a worse decision to put myself out of my misery. I will plan the move tomorrow. I will go live in a third world country, or an island, or somewhere remote? I don't think I can face the patronizing comments behind my back, the slanderous defamation in the media, and the scathing mortification of it all. Sleep will be my only refuge from the torment. I pop some 5Htp and a few Ibuprofen PMs, turn off my phones, and do my best to crash. Lights out.

* * *

I wake with the biggest migraine, and for a second I think I just had a very bad dream. You know when you wake up suddenly, and it takes a moment to realize you are at home, safe in your own bed, and you breathe a sigh of relief. Yeah, well, this moment is the opposite.

I cruise through the place and discover that no one is home as I go to the kitchen to make some coffee. There will be no Starbucks today. I'm not leaving the house.

I momentarily open the door to grab the *LA Times* leaning against it in the hallway and hear a few flashes. Somehow just like a cockroach, a paparazzo got on the premises. I flip whomever the bird from behind the door and shut it.

I take another sip from my giant mug and hastily open the paper. Unbelievable. *Only in LA* would this make front headlines. It says that Tom and Ryan have been charged with four counts of murder, conspiracy to commit murder, embezzlement, coercion, fraud, and tax evasion. My name is not mentioned in that article.

In a small, related article under it, is more about the Globes' drama, but my name is in it. It states that I have been vindicated of all charges, and that by cooperating with authorities, have single-handedly brought them to justice. Yeah, right.

I turn on the TV and the post awards shows are calling me the new "Boy toy goes Bad boy." I think I am getting a great spin on this. I look at my phone, and I have received calls all night and all morning. I turn off the mute button and it starts ringing immediately. I call Cali back and she answers, "Hello, Devon!"

"Will you forgive me?"

"Don't worry about it. If you hadn't done it, I might have and that would have been much, much worse. The press thinks you were protecting me. So, it's all good. I was so worried. I wanted to talk to you all night!"

"I hope I didn't ruin your night."

"Are you kidding? You are my hero. My publicist wants me to marry you now!"

"So, can I see you?"

"We have to wait. I don't think you understand the magnitude of this thing. If you step outside your place right now, I'm sure there is a swarm, and they will follow you here where there is already a nest of them."

"Alright, Sorry. I just couldn't help it."

"Everyone understands, and you are the new good-bad boy on the block, so just accept it. I have to do another interview now. Call me later."

"Okay."

What a shitstorm of aggravating amplitude. I can't even leave to go get some milk for my coffee! So, this is what it is like to be famous. Not cool. Truly overrated.

* * *

I spend the rest of the week holed up in my crib, watching old movies and relaxing as much as possible. The last year has been a jolt on the system like never before. If I haven't aged ten years, then I've matured five maybe.

Cin brings me home food and keeps me company when she can. I try to converse with her until I start to just tune her out. Our perspectives on everything are as different as a dog and cat. Intellectual juxtaposition . . .

I try to call Cali now and then at night. According to all her foot soldiers, it seems like she wants to see me, but she is too busy taking care of business with her post-Golden Globe follow-up press. She should be. She has to capitalize on this momentum to keep her career at full speed, so I understand.

I feel out of place now though, in a bewildered state. Lost in bemusement. Lost in Life. I have decided to get out of town and rendezvous with my bro in Jamaica. Never been there, but it might be fun. I leave a bunch of uninspired phone calls and pack. I will fly out tomorrow evening.

PART III

LIBERATION

Jamaica Bound—
Beginning Silhouette
Vacation Flashback

I zip up my last piece of luggage and am ready for Cin to take me to the airport. She walks in my room and informs me there is someone at the door to see me. I tell her to tell them to "get lost."

"I don't think that's a good idea?" she says back.

I go to the door and look through the tiny peephole, and it is Cali's driver. Slightly baffled, I open the door.

"Get your things. I will take you to the airport," he orders in his authoritative, baritone voice.

"Um, okay, sure."

I bring out my stuff and hug Cin goodbye. I am riding to the airport in style. I think I am beginning to like this a little too much.

* * *

As soon as we pull away, he says, "We are stopping for a second on the way, I hope you don't mind."

"No. Do your thing. I'm fine on time."

"Thanks."

It's funny how a car ride lets you contemplate about Life, especially when you're not driving. I gaze at the passing scenery and look up at the Hollywood sign that I lived almost directly below when I first moved to this enigmatically bizarre city.

I used to sit on the roof of the building when I was practically broke, and stare at it and speculate. Hollywood was like a new land that I, the discoverer, had to find new adventure in. I had dreams and aspirations of becoming "The" trainer to the stars. "The" health consultant. "The" fitness guru.

It is the simplest ironies that seem most profound, I guess. Because as I traveled that painful, fateful journey, I lost sight of where I came from, and how far I have distanced myself from who I really was when I moved here.

I have become "LA" whether I like it or not. I am now part of it. Part of the living, breathing thing I make fun of. I am a root in the tree that gives this place Life. And I am only to be found thriving here. Here in LA, *Only in LA.*

The driver pulls over to the side of the road. It is a small, landscaped, grassy mound off of Sunset across from the Beverly Hills Hotel that no one really uses.

"You have someone who wants to see you," he calmly says.

"Thanks," I softly reply.

How ambiguously vague is that? I hesitatingly get out and feel the sun hit me. I slowly shut the door, not knowing what to expect and begin to walk towards the middle of the place.

It is dusk, and the sun is dropping in the pink and orange cloud-filled sky. I put on my sunglasses, but I still I have to squint and put my hand on my forehead to even look ahead. As I get closer, a silhouetted figure of a voluptuous woman in the center shadowed by the last remaining sunlight paces. I can see her hair flowing in the warm breeze. She looks like a—

"Would you like some more mango juice?" the waitress asks me.

"Oh . . . Yeah, Ya Mon."

She takes my cup as my bro gives me an inquisitive look from across the table and snaps his fingers.

"Hello. You alright there?"

"Um, yeah . . . Whew . . . Damn, just had the most intense flashback. Complete déjà vu. It was so surreal."

"Take a look at that walking by at about eight o'clock, and you'll be fine."

I turn to look and see her again as she passes by us, the lovely silhouette. The goddess.

"That's what started it in the first place my brotha', that's what started it all in the first place . . ."

Back from Vacation

I have been back from Jamaica for almost a month now, and I can't sleep. I try, but I still keep getting up in frustration and pace the floor. I'm just so rested, I guess.

That's not it. I think I am surprisingly restless because I have a new client tomorrow. I shouldn't be so emotionally attached to the outcome, but I want it to go perfect. So, I end up mentally rethinking everything that was taken into consideration already and ingested in my crazed head.

Ultimately, it never matters because when I get there, I just kick into autopilot, take over, and am right on target. Even when they have had a trainer before it seems to only endorse my skills. We talk, we laugh, we bond, they grimace, they sweat, no problem.

Tomorrow is the number one (C.A.A.— Creative Artists Agency) talent agent in town though. He is the kind of guy that believes that if I do an extra half-hour of cardio for him, he will actually lose weight. That it will be manifested strictly because of the intensity of his sheer will!

In other words, if any response to anything he says doesn't start with a "Y," then you are forever banished to extinction from his Life if you are not family. His family gets the "three strikes program." It is heavily rumored that even Alec Baldwin, Tom Hanks, Julia Roberts, Robert De Niro, etc. return his calls within five minutes!

He is in for a treat tomorrow though because I won't even talk to him. I just don't want to give him the privilege of opinion (or should I say take the chance), or opportunity to be controlling.

I will pretend I have laryngitis, and just show him the exercise physically first and then point for him to proceed and tap him on the shoulder when I want him to stop. He will have to cerebrally multitask to keep his big brain rollin', be able to only push his own weight around on himself, and get his poker face quietly beat up by someone else.

As I pace the floor hoping for restful sleep, I look up out of the long narrow windows of my vaulted ceiling and see the crisp full moon. I walk out on the deck, and stare like I have so many times before. It somehow puts me in a trance. I reminisce about the night adventures I have had while that golden pie was high in the sky, recollecting the steamy memories made under it like the first night I got back from Jamaica . . .

THE CALISTA REUNION II

FEBRUARY 14

I met her under the same beaming full moon for a quaint, romantic French dinner on the back patio at Café Marly's on Melrose. I was cool with the cloak and dagger dating experience at first, but on the way there, realized how silly it was to have to hide from everyone and everything when right before going to the Golden Globes she said that she "Loved me."

I valet, and stroll in to find her elegantly dressed and sitting like Queen Elizabeth in the back corner patio table, sipping a cognac and even though my brother and I had an assortment of ladies to keep us company while we were away, I sincerely missed her.

I was still smitten and wanted to skip the main course and make her dessert right then and there on top of the table. She looks at me coyly when I sit down. "You look sexy with a tropical tan."

"Thanks, you look sexy without one."

"I missed you, I have an opportunity for you and a proposition as well."

"Wow, I'm having déjà vu. Should I be excited or afraid?"

"I'm famished. Let's order some food and then we can talk business."

"Oh, so this is a business meal?"

"No, darling, I want to tear you apart, I just need to tell you a few things first."

"Okay . . ."

We order the escargot, and the highly-rated black mussels for an appetizer, and then after a few more sips of vino, and flirtatious looks, she says it, "When are you going to quit your job?"

"Excuse me?"

"You don't have to work as a trainer anymore. I can get you in the mailroom at William Morris Endeavor."

"Oh, so, I can become one of those sharks?"

She hesitates for only a second. "Well, what do you want to do?"

"Well, what would be good enough for you?"

"I just meant that you are so smart and capable of so much—"

"I don't think Bobby and Michelle care what I do as long as I spend time with them."

"Don't bring them into this!"

"Wow . . . Do you hear yourself, what we sound like? I don't know. I thought coming back would be a little bumpy but this—I didn't sign up for this. Maybe I should go?" I start to stand up.

"No. Don't make a scene or it will be on all the TV tabloids tomorrow!"

I stand up anyway. "You're worse, you've gotten worse."

"What the hell are you talking about? Sit down." She is gritting her teeth as she says this, "Please . . ."

"I . . . I just . . . can't do this." I turn to walk out.

Out of spite I walk up to the gorgeous hostess, who has been checking me out since I got there, I ask for a pen, write down my number, place it gently in her hand while coupling it with both of mine and whisper, "Call me."

She smiles and says, "Thank you, I will," in her sensuous French accent.

I never looked back but Cali must have been livid. In the space of five weeks, she had become unbearably controlling already. This was just the tip of the iceberg, I'm sure.

Either that, or my glowing, relaxed aura from the Caribbean was not up to the LA squeeze yet. I was still on that free-for-all vacation high. Reality would hit later, I suppose, but for now I was just riding the carefree wave of no-stress pacification.

* * *

I get about one hundred feet from the restaurant in my car when my cell starts to play the downloaded ringtone "Classic Man" by Jidenna. I answer, "Ho la."

She quickly blurts out, "I'm sorry."

"Me too, you seem different Cali."

"Please meet me somewhere else private, I want you."

I can't help but think back to the old Beverly Hills/Hollywood Housewife booty call days and wonder. Am I a fool repeating his folly? Then I start to grin. I guess I will have my cake and eat it too. "Where?"

"Go to bungalow 733 at the Beverly Hills Hotel in twenty, I have a surprise for you."

"A'ight."

"See you there."

* * *

I arrive and casually find the outside door. I am either

going to get a night of passionate hardcore, makeup sex, or jumped by her new bodyguards she prowls around with now.

I knock. No lights on either. I look at the number again and am about to leave when the door swings open, and a naked leg curls around the doorframe from behind it for only a few seconds and then instantly disappears.

I walk in, close the door, and turn around to see she is wearing her ivory birthday suit, and a big red bow across her navel. She purrs, "Happy Valentine's Day, untie your present and play with it." I reach for the bow and as I grab hold of a loose end, she saunters away to the bed and it unravels and falls to the floor. I see her heart-shaped derrière as she leans over to reach for a glass of champagne by the bed.

After handing it to me, I courteously take a sip and stand there like a statue, and smile. Suddenly, she vigorously grabs the glass, drops it on the floor, pushes me on the bed, and starts kissing me all over.

The night was one of the best yet. Ever. I think we made up some new positions that I haven't seen in my Karma Sutra book. It was not Tantric either, it was "spank me harder" sex, but that's all it was. The Love we once had was gone. It was heavy petting, and it was so hot, but it was over. The next morning, she was already gone. The note on the pillow said, "Until next time, Thanx!"

A New Dawn—
The Guru Chick

February 22

I finally drift off to slumberland, only to feel like I just got there when the two alarms I set both sound off. It's Monday, and time to get forced back into reality, Hollywood style. I am still in a haze from the time off and need two cups of coffee to bring me up to speed. I was going to try to switch to green tea again, but it just doesn't fuel the jet like the java.

I have already finished with the C.A.A. Talent Agent I was losing sleep over the night before. Ironically, of course, it was a walk in the park. He was a pussycat. He doesn't scare me at all. Maybe his reputation is a little exaggerated, huh. Probably one of those, "it's better to rule by fear type" executives. I was surprised at his level of determination though. I now have a new appreciation for where he is at, and how hard he must have worked to get there. He will be a great client.

* * *

My oldest client is warming up on the treadmill now. Remember the investment banker I met my first day in Hollyweird, who now is my oldest local client? Well, he is a billionaire now, and pays me triple my fee to keep him in line. He is returning for the summer from Europe, and back in town to toss some money at a documentary filmmaker for the Democratic Party.

This guy doesn't shine on to too many people. I happen to be one of them. He is cynical, dark, and poker-faced in mixed company. Very sharp but seldom speaks.

You would never know he is so wealthy until he walks over to his personal jet at the airport in Van Nuys when you drop him off near the tarmac after he nonchalantly asks you for a ride because he doesn't drive. It is just one example of why he is viewed as eccentric to the bone, but his commonality for such a man of his stature is what I find most endearing about him.

He reminds me of Orson Welles in the old, black and white *Citizen Kane* movie, but I am going to call him Jack. The man who climbed the beanstalk to riches but found the giant at the top was really his own demons.

Jack is almost done warming up on the treadmill and is looking pissed off as usual. I haven't seen him for quite a while, but he barely cracks a smile as he mutters, "Good morning."

He called me while I was gone and said he had only gained a few pounds, but he looks like he either had some dinner with his salt last night, or he has been boozing it up. His face is so red and bloated it practically looks swollen like he just had plastic surgery a few days ago.

He says his blood pressure is up, and I have to hold back when I want to say, "No shit," as if I can't tell. He was on the wagon the last time we met. I suppose that's over, and he is back to trying to find an answer, or something, at the bottom of a bottle again.

I didn't expect this. I thought he was going to his regular AA meetings and was going to surprise me with his new, improved self. Great, my first, full workweek back, and this is what my Monday is morphing into already.

I smile and ask, "So how's your diet?"

His face goes sour for a second, but he stops walking, looks me in the eye, and unloads. "It needs some work, and before you ask, I had my last drink last night for the next three months alright, it's time to get in shape again. My anniversary is coming up. I don't want to be served papers and pay half, so this time I am committed kid. Whatever it takes, just don't give up on me!"

"I won't, let's go."

I know trainers who have fired clients before. It is rare, but I have seen a couple of really good ones in LA do it. They don't play. If you drop the ball, then it's over. Today, I feel like maybe I should adopt this policy.

If I fire him though, I am letting him down. He is counting on me to help him. To be the one person in his Life that he trusts and can depend on to be positive and sincerely tell him he can do it. I want to wash my hands of him, but I just can't. He reminds me of one of those guys on the street who was one step away from keeping it all together if only someone would have had just an ounce more compassion for him.

Okay, maybe vacation made me soft. No, it's the new Devon. The hybrid of the old and the new! The more caring and devoted one I once again vowed to be on the beach, as I watched the sunset at the farthest west end of the island. I have been quickened once more. It's great to be back, back in the City of Angels, *Only in LA.*

As time has passed, so has my health concerns, but it is time to adjust my back and my meridians. I do the one-stop-shop on San Vicente. First it is crack, crack, crack, pop, and I am standing straighter. Then I walk out the door and across the hallway for my second appointment with Miss Guru Chick.

It has been a while, so she practically bear hugs me when I walk in the door. She says my face looks "softer," and that I have "good energy," until I lay down and she starts to "assess me within" just like old times.

Once again, I am astonished by how she does this, and knows where to put those needles to improve my energy flow, when she suddenly steps back as if she is startled, and it scares me.

"What's wrong?" I say surprised, since this has never happened before.

She looks at me, and in slow motion, a huge revelatory smile overcomes her face. "You have had some real growth my friend. I think the darkness I felt before has been overcome by new light."

"Um, well, what does that—"

"I am trying to say your heart has healed since I last saw you."

Happy with this, but inquisitively befuddled as to what else there is to say I reply, "C'mon, so you don't have any advice to give a healed man?"

She softly touches my forehead with the palm of her hand, tilts her head and says with dignity, "Prepare for Life like you prepare for a meeting with God."

I mentally flashback to the Jamaican-sunset prayer moment I had on vacation, and can't help but crack a gigantic grin at her and mischievously respond, "So, to wear cologne, or to not wear cologne, that is the question?"

She laughs and says, "It is time to go."
Yes, it is time to go . . .

Journey to be continued . . .

ACKNOWLEDGMENTS

I am hereby putting complete faith in God and the Universe by expressing this.

About the Author

Have you ever heard of LA gym culture? Where the celebs go to get that sexy lower rectus abdominus love muscle to pop out with that private trainer, and wonder what goes on behind all the repetitions, relationships, eccentricities, huffing and puffing, and sweat? Hello, my name is Eric Jorgensen. I am a poet, a writer, and a certified professional trainer. I have been living in Hollywood for over a decade, and I love my profession. I have had the pleasure of meeting and experiencing a wonderful array of characters and personalities throughout the years that have influenced my own perception of Los Angeles and the preoccupation with health and fitness that is so prevalent in this city.